JERICHO

CLUB ENVY BOOK ONE

Donna R. Mercer

Sassy Writer Publishing

Cover by Nikki Crescent at Honeyhut Designs
Interior Design by Breakout Designs
Editor: Crystol Wiedeman

ISBN -10 1974145301
ISBN -13 978-1974145300

Dedication

In Loving Memory of

Mildred D. Norris

SpringLea Ellorien Henry

Thanks to everyone who help to make this book a reality.
Avalon Gridley
Arika Mercer
Nicole Norris

Coming Soon in Series
Brandon coming in 2017
Lathan coming in 2017
Sebastian coming in 2017

Sign up for Newsletter to keep informed of new releases and make sure to join my Facebook Group to stay up-to-date on contests and free giveaways.

TABLE OF CONTENTS

CHAPTER ONE

JERICHO RYDER STOOD on the balcony looking out over the dance floor.

This level of the club was crammed full of people writhing and gyrating to the heavy bass playing throughout this level of the club. Jericho's club, Club Envy, catered to most musical tastes. Should a customer change floors, so too would the genre change. Club Envy didn't just gear things towards one taste, it encompassed all types of music. This is how Jericho managed to stay on top of the ever-changing club industry.

Jericho was the billionaire owner of the hottest club to be found in Colorado Springs. Clients were willing to wait for hours, in the unbelievable lines just to pass the velvet rope, into one of the most exclusive clubs in Colorado.

Winter, Fall, Summer, Spring. Snow, rain, or sunshine. They waited to enter. After all, if you wanted to be one of the young, hot elites, you were seen in Club Envy.

Done surveying the club, Jericho took the stairs down to the lower level. Down to a part of the building the average club goers didn't even know existed. To enter this part of the club, you needed to be on the global rich list for starters. But even that didn't guarantee you entrance, you also had to be referred by a current member.

Occasionally guest passes were given to women to mix things up in the clientele. It was a necessary part of the club business. Where the women went the men would follow. A fact Jericho catered to as it raised profits. But as with the men the women also met a higher standard.

Class was the key word. It was not a looks thing. Being classy trumped appearances. If they didn't possess an iota of class then they would be escorted from the premises.

After all, ratchetness destroyed many nightclubs.

The bouncer guarding the door nodded respectfully to Jericho as he entered the most exclusive part of the club. He did not demand respect, he earned it, along with the loyalty of his employees. Jericho provided good wages, a safe work environment and benefits that made it difficult to leave. His employees knew they would not be able to find such a good work balance anywhere else.

The door closed behind him. Malcolm, the concierge for this level, greeted him. It was Malcolm's job to cater to the demands and whims of the exclusive club goers within.

Malcolm determined who belonged in the exclusive part of the club and who did not meet the standard enough to so much as cross the threshold.

"Good evening Mr. Ryder." Malcom always reminded him of one those fastidious butlers you pictured manning the mansions in the most expensive part of town. He dressed to the nines with not a hair out of place. In fact, Jericho thought his hair was too well trained to dare to move without Malcolm's direction.

Jericho didn't know how he ended up in the Springs and

working for him. Malcom story belonged to him and Jericho didn't much care. All that mattered to him was that Malcom did his job and he did it well.

"Evening, Malcolm, how are things tonight?" Jericho always maintained vigilance of the area should problems come up that he needed to handle. It was unusual for a problem to need his personal attention, especially in Malcom's capable hands. Just in case though, he always wanted to be available.

"Things are well. We have high rollers in attendance." Malcolm gestured to several of the curtained off VIP sections where there was a constant flow of waitresses in their haute couture uniforms.

Malcolm pointed out several groups among the already elite clientele, indicating just what level of society he was talking about.

"Ahhhh. I see Sheik Hasaan is looking to add to his harem." He mentally started tallying the tab the Arab playboy and his entourage would rack up. Yes, it was definitely going to be a profitable night.

"Yes, indeed he is. Unfortunately, one of the waitresses is overstepping the boundaries between good service and *good services*." Malcolm put an emphasis on the last two words. Malcolm would never be crass enough to point out when a female was on the hunt for an easy paycheck. He, like all the employees knew the number one rule for working at Club Envy: Absolutely no fraternizing with the clients. Relationships made in club rarely lasted beyond a few nights. The future business interactions within the club became stinted and awkward. This caused problems for him and the rest of his staff.

"Get rid of her then. Give her the standard severance pay and tell her that her services will no longer be needed."

It might have sounded cold, but Jericho was running a club not a dating service. Malcolm gave a nod of understanding and he knew the matter would be handled discretely and professionally.

"The winner of the charity raffle is in attendance tonight with a couple of her friends." Malcolm gestured to the gold and white VIP section occupied by three females. He watched them giggling over one of the club's signature shots. A body shot off of Marco's muscular chest, it was a popular item.

"Okay, I will be sure to stop by and congratulate them."

He had donated the VIP experience to a silent auction for a children's charity. This was all part of his program for giving back to the community. It was his way of paying it forward. Jericho made a point of doing so, he always remembered the help he received for college, which got him out of the not-so-nice Denver suburb where he'd grown up.

When most people thought of Colorado they thought of the small towns and farmland. They forgot about the big cities existing in Colorado along with the big city problems, just like L.A., Chicago, and Miami. Denver may not be as big as those cities, but it was on its way to the same disparity of neighborhoods. It was not just minority kids growing up in rough rundown neighborhoods.

There truly was nothing worse than growing up lily-white in a neighborhood filled with black and Hispanic children and being taught the white man is your problem. Hello! He grew up just as poor if not poorer than most.

"Ensure they have a good time and they don't have any unwelcome attention." He discretely gestured to the Sheik. His habit of not wanting to take "No" for an answer from the women he deemed not to be in his social class could cause problems. After all you really couldn't trust a guy who states, "I like my coffee strong and my women weak." Any man that was afraid of a strong woman was missing out on something special in life. Jericho had a personal dislike for men who view strong women, such as his mother, as being beneath him. Any woman who was able to single-handedly raise a boy into a man and keep him out of a life of crime or gangs was not only a strong woman, she was superwoman.

Oh well, what could he say? Money doesn't buy home training.

Everything seemed to be under Malcolm's control, Jericho discretely toured the club to get the mood of the crowd. He paused in his path when Delicious, the lead singer of the girl group *The Sex Kittens*, draped herself across his shoulders, long blonde hair swaying with her every movement.

"Hello handsome." her singing voice was a lot different from her speaking voice. Through the grapevine, rumors of help from autotune abound. He honestly wasn't sure what music magic had been performed to enhance her tone. He just knew that her speaking voice reminded him of a heavy smoker.

"Hello Delicious." he gave her a one-armed hug as he pressed a kiss to her temple. He swore he could feel all of her ribs as he hugged her. Personally, he preferred women with a little bit of meat on her bones, apposed to society's norm of excessively thin women. He could feel her surgically enhanced breasts pressing into his side. They only part of her that appeared to have any sustenance.

He had taken her to dinner, not too long ago, thinking that there was more to her than just a desire to find a rich husband to support her. The evening had been truly miserable. Jericho had quickly determined that they had nothing in common. Delicious had spent the time talking about herself and her career. That in of itself would have been fine, but she was quick to inform him of his role in her future and that was not something they agreed on. He had to claim an early morning flight to avoid hurting her feelings when he refused to return with her to her apartment.

From that night forward he did everything in his power to avoid her. He had not returned her phone calls or text messages. He had even gone so far as to change his phone number. Whenever he encountered her in Club Envy, he was polite to her, but no more than he was to the other female guests. Still she seemed to persist, soon he was going to have to do something about her determination to see them as a couple.

"Are you having a good time, beautiful?" She shivered at the sound of his deep voice. He swore he could feel her heart beating through her ribs, but he ignored it.

Jericho knew he could convince her into bed with him if the mood struck him, even after his rejection. He was not only a billionaire, but fate had seen fit to grace him with good looks as well. He was the essence of tall, dark and handsome. Never one to neglect his own health, he had his own regular workout routine, which gave him well defined muscles. Add the thick black hair gifted to him by his mother that women couldn't resist running their hands through it.

Case in point. Delicious' left hand tangled in his hair, tugging his head down so she could reach his mouth. Jericho gently pulled back while he removed her hand from his hair. He pressed a kiss to the back of her claw tipped hand that he captured.

Seemed the most important aspect about him, to all women such as Delicious, was that he was rich. She was an up and coming artist with her group, but the word gold-digger came to mind whenever he conversed with her. Unfortunately, it was not uncommon that women seemed to cling to him, even after his rejection. In part, this was due to his reputation.

Jericho's reputation as a playboy mostly came about because he owned Club Envy. What most of them didn't know, was that he was actually very picky about his playmates. He made sure they knew up front anything with him was short term. To prevent hard feelings, he gifted them with jewels, furs and expensive trips. Delicious had been angling to become one of his playmates for quite a while with long term on her mind, but the dollar signs in her eyes told him she saw him as a permanent meal ticket. That just was not his style.

Jericho watched as she licked her lips, not the least bit attracted to her. He knew, despite his rejection, that she still believed he had fallen under her spell. If she only knew his background, then she would realize her tricks and antics were not fooling him. Perhaps then she would not waste her time on him. She could search for an easier pigeon to pluck. He gave her hand back to her and gave her a gentle slap on the ass. With a wink of the eye and a slow smile, he moved to continue his review and to greet more club goers, missing the way her face darkened in anger.

CHAPTER TWO

KELLISTA ANTHONY WAS beyond nervous. She had never done anything like this before in her life. Yes, she had done everything else in life. Getting married, raising her boys, taking care of her home, yet what did that get her?

Nothing, but gray hair. Henry, the man who said he would love her forever really meant to say, "I will love you until my next wife is born and graduates from preschool."

It was easy to tell, even now, she was still a little bitter. She expected to grow old with the love of her life, instead, she just grew old. Kellista did what most newly divorced women did. She got a new hairstyle. She packed her shit and moved the hell out of Denver and headed south. In fact, she moved to Colorado Springs where the population of other black people consisted of a total of three.

That was her note to all young women out there: Men will use you up and then trade you in for a newer model once their legacy, in the name of their children, grow up and move on.

Now the sassy redhead that the new Kellista became pulled the slinky new dress over her head and smoothed it down the voluptuous curves that she earned thru three pregnancies and a love affair with chocolate.

She didn't care if thin was in, she was a sexy bitch! The deep red dress looked absolutely luscious against her dark brown skin and thank the lord for whoever invented the built-in bra because the girls were defying gravity.

She stood in front of the full-length mirror in her new bedroom, slipping on stilettos as her cellphone started ringing. Not halting the assessment of herself in the mirror, she glanced at her phone. She couldn't stop the grin that took over her face at the sight of her older sister's phone number. She answered it to hear a southern belle voice come through the phone.

"Well hello, dahling." her older sister Cynthia had attended a historically black college in the South. There she met the love of her life and stayed to raise her family. From the sound of her voice, you would not know that she spent her formative years in Denver, Colorado. She sounded like a genteel southern belle born and bred.

"Well hello, darling." Kellista teased back at her making sure to put the emphasis on her "R".

"You ready to go out and get you some new man candy?" she asked totally ignoring her teasing like she always did when Kellista made fun of her accent.

"I don't know if I should do this?" Kellista put her on speaker phone so she could continue to fiddle with her outfit. Her earlier confidence seemed to evade her.

"Why not?" the soft spoken southern belle was gone in an instant. In its place was the hard-nose college professor that grew up on the mean streets of Denver.

"I am too old to be trolling the bar for a man." she

stated her concern with the evening out loud.

"Oh, dahling," the southern belle was back, "you are too hung up on your age. This is all that beast Henry's fault. Him marrying a kindergartner has made you feel like you're too old to start over." Older sisters have a knack for hitting problems right on the head. "What you need to do is to find you a younger man, say someone in their twenties, we want to make sure he has gone through puberty, and have him show you what you have been missing with the despicable thing you called a sex life with Henry. What? Did you only have sex with him three times? Getting pregnant with each of the boys?"

"Wow, you went there." Kellista was astounded by the things that could come out of her older sister's mouth. Usually it was her twin Caleigh that used the blunt tool method of problem solving.

"What can I say? You need some tough love. Send me a picture of your outfit." Cynthia demanded.

She took a selfie in the full-length mirror and sent it to her.

"Oh yeah, that will get you laid." Kellista rolled her eyes at her comment.

"I am not trying to get laid."

"Not with that attitude. Now make sure you flash plenty of cleavage and rope you in a young hot stud that can go all night long. Ta-ta dahling." She hung up before Kellista could respond.

Sisters. Though after the conversation, her anxiety lessened about hitting the club scene. Kellista had never been clubbing before, especially since she married young. Now with her divorce she was adjusting to being a single woman in a new day and age. All of the strict morals she been raised with went out the window years ago. It was a new world, and she didn't know how to date in this day and age. If she was speaking truthfully, she didn't know how to date in any day and age.

Her cellphone started ringing again. She expected it to be her other sister Caleigh, but she was surprised to see that it was her son, Jeremy, instead. Their relationship suffered since her divorce and his father's remarriage.

"Hello, Jeremy." she insisted to herself that this conversation would start off on a positive note.

"Mother." came the formal response. Okay, perhaps kill the positive note, she just hoped it ended without her committing a felony.

"Yes, Jeremy?"

"Aunt Caleigh told Janet that you were going to a bar tonight." He stated.

"Yes dear, I am going out with co-workers to Club Envy." she continued to apply make-up to her face. She didn't like to wear much, but she did want to highlight her eyes.

"Mother, you do realize that Club Envy is a meat market and you will not meet anyone there appropriate to your age or social standing." Oh boy. How did she raise such an ass?

"I am not looking for a date dear. I am going to spend time with my co-workers and this is the place they wanted to go. As you know, good manners dictate that the inviter chooses the place."

"Well, don't do anything inappropriate that will come back to embarrass me or father. Men in those places are looking for one thing and one thing only." That does it. It was time to pull out the big guns in the form of her mom voice and end this conversation.

"Jeremy, you seem to forget two simple facts. One, I am a grown adult and you don't dictate my actions. And two, I could give a flying fuck about embarrassing you or your father. Neither of you were concerned about embarrassing me when he was caught having an affair with an intern younger than you. If I choose to fuck the whole Denver football team on the fifty-yard line in their stadium, I expect you and your father to stand on the sideline cheering me on." she took a page from Cynthia's book and hung up the phone before he could say anything further.

"Fucking ungrateful brat." she muttered. Oops, she used the f-word. Her bible thumping, intern humping ex-husband would be having a fit. "Only vulgar women use foul language." That was one of his favorite sayings.

Kellista was happy with the choices she made after divorcing Henry. With her part of their old house she had been able to afford a newer, smaller house in a nice neighborhood in the Springs. She had been a little bitter when she bought it. She made sure that it was only big enough for "me, myself, and I". She did this to prevent her "I am grown" children from coming to live with her if something went wrong with their perfect life. Instead they would be required to go stay with their father and his new spouse Bambi. Or was it Candi with an I? Like she gave a flying fuck. Oops! She did it again, Brittany knew she could make a song.

Regardless those ungrateful boys that she birthed could shack up with their father when something happens to cause things to swirl around the toilet bowl of life. Let them live with their father and "isn't our new stepmom awesome."

"Well FUCK you, Henry" she could not stop herself from giggling. Kellista felt the last of the tension in her shoulders release.

She added a dash of red lipstick. Look out men of Colorado Springs, this cougar was on the prowl tonight. "Rawr!" another set of giggles escaped her at that sound.

Chapter Three

AS THE NIGHT progressed, Kellista was having a great time. The girls she came with, April and Nancy, were two women she met at her new job. When they invited her to Club Envy she hadn't quite believed them. Even she had heard of this club, from her middle son, he'd been trying to get in for months. It was famous worldwide. You needed to know somebody, who knew somebody, WHO KNEW SOMEBODY to even get into the club.

April was someone who knew somebody. Her brother-in-law's company purchased the VIP package as part of a children's auction. He was going to surprise her sister with a night on the town. Instead her sister surprised him with the announcement of expecting their fourth child. They gave the tickets to April while they celebrated the addition to their family in a familiar way. Trying to make baby number five. So that was how April ended up invited her co-workers and here they were, having the night of their lives.

The girls' feelings of excitement was catching. Kellista lit up the dance floor moving her body in ways she wasn't even aware it could move when she was younger let alone at the grand old age of forty-seven. Several different men asked to dance, but she turned them down to continue partying with the girls.

April pointed out some famous singer named Delicious. Experiencing the club was far more exciting than Kellista expected.

The elegance of the club was something she'd never experienced before. Soon enough, her energy declined, so she decided to reclined on the soft fabric covered divan, instead watching April and Nancy taking body shots off of Marco their private bartender. Yes, that's right they had their very own bartender and he was hot as hell. Damnit there goes her potty mouth.

"Oh my…" she realizing the words slipped past her lips as she watched the gorgeous specimen approach the VIP tent. She never actually looked at other men that closely before. She had grown up with Henry, they knew their families wished they would marry. She never dated, and regretted the missed the opportunity to look around at other men as a single female. Perhaps if she had, she would have known that there was a lot better out there then Henry. Such as the approaching gorgeous specimen of manhood demonstrated. He was taller than her. He had thick black hair that curled on the ends. The tailored trousers hugged powerful thighs and an ass that was good enough to bite. Nice and firm. Kellista unconsciously licked her lips at the sight of him.

A tailored low collar shirt hugged a pair of broad shoulders and clung tightly to his chest and stomach. She looked up into his face and saw the slow smile that crossed his face as he caught her checking him out. She actually whimpered at the sight. That smile was not fighting fair. Womankind would not be able to survive anything so devastating.

She shrugged.

The old her would have blushed and stammered an apology, but the new Kellista just said "Fuck it!" and enjoyed the view.

Eyes that blue should be outlawed she thought as she nibbled on her bottom lip.

"Hello, ladies." Wow, the perfect package had a sexy voice. He spoke to the three of them, though his eyes did not leave Kellista. He took in every aspect of her body as she reclined on the divan sipping her cocktail. Cock, she giggled at the word. He probably sported a very large one by the sight of the bulge in his pants.

"I am Jericho Ryder. Owner of Club Envy and I wanted to make sure you are having a good time." He looked away from her. Kellista slowly released her breath.

She hadn't even notice that she was holding it. He picked up April's hand and placed a kiss on the back of it as she introduced herself. He repeated the gesture with Nancy.

She watched as he skirted the table to approach her. Kellista held out her hand as if she was the Queen of Egypt greeting her subject, expecting him to kiss the back of it as he did with the other two.

Her mouth dropped in surprise as he turned it over and placed a lingering kiss on the palm of her hand.

Such an intimate gesture.

She couldn't stop the shivers that shot through her arm and straight to her pussy. Her nipples grew hard.

This response was new to her.

Her relationship with Henry consisted of a long slow warm up and usually a lingering burn that lasted long after he finished. The sudden heat and attraction were new feelings and she was not quite sure she understood them.

To add a little distance, she carefully sat up.

However, Jericho didn't let go of her hand.

She felt at a distinct disadvantage laying down on the divan.

"Hello, darling." the sexy, deep voice once again caught her off guard as the man spoke. It felt like a smooth caress, increasing the shivers to her pussy. He took her sitting up as an invitation to sit down next to her on the divan. Personal space was not in his vocabulary.

He sat close enough that his right side was plastered against Kellista's left side from knee to shoulder. There was no space in-between them.

He did not let go of her hand. It surprised her, the warmth, it had been a long time since someone held her hand like that. The last time someone held her hand, it was her boys, before they grew up and determined that holding your mom's hand was not cool. This had a very distinctly different feeling.

Jericho ignored the subtle tugging she did as he turned back to April and Nancy.

"If there is anything that you need, be sure to let Marco know. That way he can get it for you." She barely heard him, her focus on her hand. His grip was firm and warm, a feeling of safety encompassed her. She examined him up-close noticing the tattoo behind his right ear. She wondered what woman marked him as hers. A small pang of disappointment hit her heart at the thought that it was not her.

Woo, baby what?

He was half her age, or at least the same age of her sons. It hit her then that she was lusting after a younger man. Maybe she was no better than her cradle robbing ex-husband, lusting after children? She couldn't blame alcohol for such feelings.

She could hear her sister Cynthia's voice yelling "Go for it!"

"I hope you don't mind if I steal your friend here?" that caught her attention as she tuned back into the conversation.

"Sure, go ahead," April smirked in response, "just be sure to return her in one piece by closing time. We still want to take her home with us." She gaped in disbelief at April.

Jericho stood up and tugged her along with him, before leading her out of the VIP tent. He gripped his prize firmly. She followed behind, too startled to react.

She mouthed the words "Help me!" to April and Nancy. They just stood there smirking at her as they mouthed, "Lucky Bitch!" back at her. She changed her mind about these girls. They were not her friends after all.

CHAPTER FOUR

JERICHO COULD NOT believe the luscious prize that he found in his very own club. Laying there on that divan just waiting to be eaten like the finest delicacy. His heart almost stopped at how beautifully her dark skin contrasted with the divan.

He had never been so glad he went with his instinct to purchase it and plan the VIP tent around it.

The red dress hugged her curves, emphasizing her generous breasts. Everything about her was delectable, but the piece de resistance was her face. Soulful brown eyes with the hint of feistiness.

Even harder to resist was the hidden passion in her gaze when her eyes examined his body. He had instantly felt heat at that gaze. In his experience only women with a wild side wore red lipstick. It took a certain amount of passion to wear the color red on your lips with confidence.

Oh how his bedmate for the night wore it well. Rules were flexible for him as the club owner, and since she was not a regular clientele he felt no hesitation in what he was about to do.

Especially, if she didn't stop nibbling on that bottom lip of hers. He would not be responsible for what happened when he lost his mind.

He led her through the crowds to his private office. A quiet place would be the perfect location to get to know her better. Oh, how he fully intended to know her, very well.

As soon as the door closed behind her, her wide eyes scanned around his office. Probably trying to find an exit to get away from him. There was another exit, but that would be his little secret for now.

"Would you like a drink?" She shook her head. Then cocked it to one side as she studied him.

"What are you? Twelve, thirteen years old?" She inquired in what she may have thought was a stern mom voice but it just made her hotter in his eyes. Adorable more than stern.

A laugh escaped him, "I am thirty-two." he clarified, smiling charmingly at her.

"Oh god, I could be your mother." She moaned pacing around his office. He watched her butt sway in those sexy heels. He wondered if she realized that each step she took only excited him further. He imagined the feel of those legs wrapped around him, those sexy stiletto in the air as he touched the smoothness of her skin.

Oh yeah, that moan was a sound he wanted to hear.

Preferably when his head was firmly between her thighs. Either head would be fine at this point. Either one would bring them both satisfaction. It was rare for him to feel such an immediate attraction, but he fully intended to take advantage of it.

He pulled her closer, into his arms, "Yeah, you could be, but you're not. My mother is alive and well and living on a beach in Florida." he told her right before capturing her mouth.

A groan of excitement escaped him. She proved his assumption right. Those luscious lips tasted amazing. His tongue gently danced across them until she parted them and allow him entrance.

Deepening the kiss, he dominated her mouth, she tasted of ripe peaches, juicy and succulent, this only served to excite a craving for more.

Her soft moans of pleasure started to reach his ears. He delved deeper within her, exploring every inch. One taste was not enough. His tongue tangled with hers as he stamped her as his. Her hands snaked up to his head, burrowing into his hair, desperately pulling him closer to her. When he felt they both needed air, he pulled back, softly speaking into her ear, "I would like to know your name." he whispered to her as he planted kisses on her shoulder and neck.

"Kellista. Kellista Anthony." she moaned.

"If you would like me to stop, you only need to ask, Kellista Anthony." he gave her the faint warning, looking her in the face. Her brown eyes met his blue ones. It would kill him if she told him to stop, but he would do so. Despite his need, he was willing to do whatever she asked of him. Within reason of course. Stopping he would do, leaving her was not an option. The spark between them, meant she was his, and he meant to keep her.

An uncertain look crossed her face. Jericho held his breath preparing for her answer. "No." she said. Jericho closed his eyes trying to hid the disappointment in his gaze.

"No!" she groaned rubbing her pussy against his cock, pulling his head down to her mouth, capturing his mouth with hers, "Don't stop."

Relief rushed through Jericho at her answer. Now he didn't have to test the strength of his willpower to let her go.

Jericho walked her backwards towards his desk not breaking the contact between them, one goal on his mind: getting her splayed out on his desk so that he could continue his feast.

Nothing else mattered.

As she trembled beneath him, with his dominance ensured, he slowly began traveling her body with his hands. Slowly, sensually he worked her dress over her hips touching her silky-smooth skin. Sliding his hands, a little lower, he gripped her generous ass, pulling her tight against his hard and throbbing cock.

A certain feeling of possessiveness overcame him, he thought 'Her curves are mine!' Such a feeling of possessiveness was foreign to him, but he instinctively knew that there was no way he was letting her go.

He stopped moving before they bumped into his desk. He slowly raised his mouth from hers licking his lips at the lingering taste on his tongue. The sight of her lips even plumper from his kiss made his blood boil.

He swept an arm across his desk sending everything crashing to the floor. He easily lifted her up and placed her thong-covered ass on the cool surface.

The skirt of her dress bunched up around her waist.

Grabbing the offending garment between him and his prize, he pulled her dress off and over her head. His gaze landed on her large breasts, watching her nipples tighten as the cool air of the office hit them. His mouth needed to be on those beautiful dark nipples. They reminded him of the finest blackcurrant berries.

He needed to taste them.

He laid her back on his desk his hand sliding over the

soft skin of her stomach, he pulled her legs around his waist. She moaned, eyes closed in pleasure as his cock rested snuggly against her thinly covered pussy.

She deepened the sound as he took one of her nipples into his mouth.

Kellista couldn't halt the steady stream of moans as she melted under the attention lavished upon her. She couldn't stop her hands from grasping his head and pulling Jericho closer to her breast. A whimper escaped her when he let her nipple pop out of his mouth. She had never experienced such heat building inside her.

She burned. Jericho's mouth had started a slow, hot burn, his touch only providing temporary release. She needed him inside, she could imagine what his member, separated from her only by his pants, would feel like inside her. The thought sent pulses through her.

Jericho was not stopping like she thought, no he switched to her other nipple. "I can't neglect this one." he blew on her other nipple and watched it tighten up before he raked his tongue across the nub. Kellista's body jerked up off the desk getting close to the source of such pleasure. She didn't realize she was so responsive, never before had her nipples been so sensitive.

She was gently pushed back onto the desk. Jericho's mouth never leaving her nipple. She could feel his cock rubbing up and down her moist slit. It felt huge, she wanted to see it, touch it, feel it inside her.

Jericho raised his head from her breasts and looked into her passion-filled eyes.

His hands glowed against the beauty of her skin, the contrast not only exotic, but highly erotic. Jericho would explode soon if he didn't enter her.

She was wet. He could feel her juices through the lace

thong that still covered her pussy as she grinded it against his covered cock.

He took her legs from around his waist, running his hand up them from thigh to ankle. He rested her legs against his shoulders her stiletto covered feet dangled in the air.

She was perfect now.

He planted kiss along the inside of her legs.

"More!" she moaned. He reached down and tore the flimsy cover from her pussy. His fingers ran over her drenched slit. Her neatly trimmed pussy, was a beautiful sight for him to explore, but he needed his pants off, now. Jericho removed his hand from Kellista's wet pussy to reach for the fastening of his trousers. His hardened, throbbing cock made it difficult getting the zipper down. He refused to let anything, even that, stand in the way of sinking deep within her.

Finally, the damn pants were undone. He didn't bother to remove them all the way. He was too anxious to feel Kellista's pussy wrapped around his cock. She sucked in her breath at the sight of his cock.

"I don't think it will fit." she whispered.

He rubbed his cock up and down her slick pussy. "You can take it." He said confidently. He was glad she was not one of those women who thought a pussy bare of hair was attractive. Only little girls were hairless and he was not a pedophile. The friction of her trimmed hair against his cock made him impossibly harder.

Kellista couldn't stop moaning as Jericho rubbed his cock up and down her throbbing pussy. He was much larger than her ex-husband. She cried out when he started squeezing her clit. She was the only one to ever touch her clit. Henry would never have thought of doing something so simple as touching her there. Jericho gave Kellista's clit a sharp pinch. Before she could cry out at the pain he fully sheathed himself in her body. The cry of pain turned to a moan of desire. He stroked her clit in apology.

She felt so full with him inside her, the new experience exhilarating as she tightened her legs around him. He filled her to the brim. Her whimper when he pulled out of her turned to a moan at the friction as he reentered her. She couldn't stop the cries that escaped her as Jericho fucked her, plunging deep inside.

"Yes, yes, yes!" She chanted at him as he pounded into her, she rose to meet him with every stroke. The experience was exhilarating. The feelings intoxicating. It was better than anything she had felt before.

Jericho reached up and moved Kellista's legs until her ankles crossed behind his head. He grabbed her around the thighs, lifting her from the desk surface, changing the angle as he continued entering her. He leaned back and thrusted his cock into her pussy. His hips moved nonstop. Each time his cock entered her he claimed her as his.

Kellista screamed at the new sensations that slammed through her pussy with each stroke of Jericho's cock. She felt his hands grasping her under the ass giving him more leverage to pound her body. She was lost to the feelings. She couldn't do more than chant Jericho's name as he fucked her into oblivion.

Stars exploded behind the eyelids she hadn't realize she'd closed. Her pussy clenched down on Jericho's cock as the orgasm overtook her. She couldn't stop herself from screaming, "Jericho!" not caring if everyone in Club Envy knew that the life was being fucked out of her. She heard Jericho's shout echo hers with one final thrust her pussy became flood with his cum.

Kellista cradled Jericho in her arms as he collapsed on top of her. His cock still buried deep in her pussy.

Words escaped him. He had never felt this possessiveness after being intimate with a woman before. The mind-blowing sex with someone who he met in Club Envy, breaking one of his cardinal rules, astonished him. Instead of feeling wrong everything felt right.

Kellista wiggled under Jericho as reality returned.

She just fucked a stranger in his office.

She just fucked a younger stranger in his office, her mind clarified for her.

Barely having caught her breath, she knew, she needed to get out of there before she compounded her mistake. She could only blame so much on the few drinks she had that evening.

She gave Jericho's shoulder a push until he lifted up to his elbows.

He is still cumming, she realized. She felt his cock jerk in her pussy sending intense spasms throughout her pussy.

He knew he was heavy on her, but he couldn't move. His cock was still jerking in her pussy. Another odd experience this evening. Extended cock shots were not his norm.

Finally, it stopped. He moved off of Kellista. He sat in one of the chairs in front of his desk, cock still out, pants down around his ankles, watching her scramble off of his desk. She stood there trying to smooth her hair down which was now a wild halo around her head thanks to his attention on the desk. He couldn't stop the masculine grin that covered his face.

She looked sexy as hell.

Jericho watched as the sexy look slowly turned to one of shock and horror. Kellista wide brown eyes met his blue ones. "What the fuck?!" escaped her.

"Yes, what a fuck." He gave her a lazy grin.

He was relaxed.

Nothing could ruin his mood. It had been a while since he had had such enjoyable sex, though he should probably pull up his pants and boxers.

Why bother? He felt his cock getting hard at the sight of Kellista standing before his desk with nothing but red stilettos on.

Sexy. His new favorite word.

She looked around frantically for her dress. She found it on the floor on top of the telephone that he swept off the desk. As she bent over to pick up the dress it gave him a view of her naked ass. It was just as delicious to see as the rest of her. Then it dawned on him as she pulled the dress over her head that she was going to make a run for it if he didn't stop her. She got the dress pulled down and around her hips and headed for the door.

He moved to follow her, but tripped over his own feet as they got tangled up in his pants. Damnit, she was going to get away. He tried tugging his pants off, but his shoes got in the way. He tried to tug them up, but his butt got in the way.

"Why is my body working against me?" he thought angrily.

"Don't go!" he called, reaching out to her as she opened the door.

Sad brown eyes looked back at him, "This was a mistake. I am sorry." She said before disappearing back into the club.

By the time he got his pants on and out the door she was lost in the crowd. He made his way over to the VIP area where her friends were partying, but they were gone and his efficient wait staff had already cleaned up the area.

He hit the wall in frustration. Jericho started to formulate a plan to track her down. First thing he would do would be to hire that private detective. He stood there making his mental list, efficient as always in his tasks, when Marco approached him.

"Hey boss." he called to get Jericho's attention over the music. It was obvious that he called him several times, but Jericho was in his own world busy making plans.

"Huh?" he looked up in surprise.

"Hey that little blonde from the VIP section asked me to give you this." he handed him a business card.

"Thanks." Jericho looked at it and clapped him on the shoulder. "Marco, you have just earned yourself a bonus." Marco looked as surprised as Jericho felt at the joy rushing through him.

In his hand, he now held a business card of one Kellista Anthony, Human Resource Manager. Finding her was too easy. He headed back to his office to formulate a plan to woo the erotic creature back into his embrace.

CHAPTER FIVE

KELLISTA RUSHED OUT of Jericho's office back towards the VIP tent that Nancy and April were waiting for her at. She couldn't stop the replay of what had just happened on his desk from running through her mind. She needed to grab her friends and leave before Jericho caught up with her. As she waded through the crowd in Club Envy her mind started processing her reaction and she realized that she was not reacting to the act of fucking Jericho on his desk. That didn't bother her, which amazed her.

No, she was still tingling over the best sexual experience in her life. The thing that she was hung up on was that Jericho was only a few years older than her oldest son. After all, her ex had done exactly the same thing, hadn't he?

She was lost in troubled thoughts when she bumped into someone. She looked up recognizing the singer that April pointed out earlier.

"Oh, excuse me." she said politely stepping to the side to go around her.

The singer, Delicious, Kellista remembered her name,

grabbed hold of her arm in a tight grip as she moved past her. She dug her nails into Kellista's arm as she pulled Kellista around to face her.

"Stay away from Jericho." the singer snarled at Kellista.

"What?" she stopped confusion crossing her face at this woman's words.

"Jericho Ryder is mine!" Delicious practically screamed, possessively, getting into Kellista's face.

Kellista pulled her arm from Delicious's grasp. Looking at the marks left by the singer from the fake nails. She might not go looking for a fight, but she was not one to walk away from one.

Kellista turned around to face Delicious squarely. She took in the expensive dress she wore, the perfectly done makeup topped off with long blonde hair extensions. Her appearance faltered further when added to the expensive boob job on a frame that was overwhelmed by them and the snarl on her face. All together it did not make an attractive picture.

She paused before reacting, catching up to what she had said. Swallowing her anger at the rude attack, Kellista apologized for her behavior "I am sorry." Having been a victim of a cheating ex, she was appalled that she'd become Jericho's unwitting accomplice.

"That's right, bitch. Know your place." The smugness rolling off of Delicious was palpable, "Besides Jericho is too much of a man for you. You're so old your pussy is probably filled with dust." At that, her anger burned back, cheating or not, she did not deserve to be spoken to that way.

"Really? That's not what Jericho was shouting a minute ago in his office." Kellista refrained from snapping her head at Delicious. It was a natural reaction left over from her days of brawling with her brothers and sisters. Her self-control stopped there, she couldn't stop the hand that settled on her hip or the finger that came up to emphasis her point.

"Listen up little girl. You are obviously Barbie doll stupid. If Jericho wanted you then he would have been with you and not me." She hadn't finished her statement before Delicious interrupted her.

"You are only a little diversion while he waits for me to finish launching my singing career." she flipped her blonde hair over her shoulder.

"You keep telling yourself that, honey. But in my experience if a man truly wanted a woman nothing would stop him from getting her."

"Listen you bitch!" Delicious's snarling face further took away from her appearance, "Jericho is my meal ticket and you don't want to get in my way. You will not like the consequences."

"No, you listen little girl. I have spanked children bigger than you before and I am not afraid to do it again. Now I would advise you to get the hell out of my way because you don't want none of this." Kellista gestured down her body before pushing past Delicious.

Steam was almost visibly coming out of Delicious's ears, but Kellista didn't have time to play games with children.

Once past Delicious, she could practically feel Jericho breathing down her neck. She glanced behind her to see if he left his offices yet, but her view was blocked by the other club goers.

Kellista spun around as her arm was grabbed again. Oh no, she already felt the bite of those claws. She shook her head; some kids didn't learn.

"He's mine you old bitch!" Delicious snarled drawing

back her free hand and swinging it towards Kellista's face.

Kellista threw up her arm blocking the fist before it got near her face. She grabbed ahold of Delicious's arm with her free hand, pulling her captured arm free. Kellista told herself not to do it, she knew that her years of training in Brazilian fighting style would place the girl at a disadvantage, but it was already too late.

Her arm now free of Delicious's hold, she bent her arm at the elbow and turned to strike Delicious with the tip of her elbow using a classic Capoeira move. She knew as soon as her elbow made contact that Delicious's nose was broken. Oops. That was not going to photograph well.

Delicious let out a loud scream. Thus, she attracted the attention of security. Kellista stepped back from her. "I told you that you didn't want any of this." She left Delicious surrounded by her entourage screaming about the "Fucking bitch that broke her nose."

She needed to get out Club Envy before Jericho managed to get his pants up and security caught up to her. Then she would figure out why she was fighting for a man she barely knew and definitely couldn't keep.

Chapter Six

KELLISTA SPENT THE Saturday morning frantically cleaning her home in the hopes that doing so would distract her from the thoughts of Jericho and the incident that occurred on his desk the night before. Every memory caused her body to flush with heat. Her heart beat faster at her wanton behavior. She deserved a one-way ticket to Hell.

No, the ghost of her mother was rearing its head waving her moral code at her. Her thoughts were much worse. Her thoughts were of how much she enjoyed the encounter, not the moral implications of the pleasure she enjoyed. Even worse, they included thoughts of when a repeat would happen.

She couldn't help it. They were some of the most sexually satisfying moments of her forty-seven years. Then she remembers the worst fact of it all, that the most sexually satisfying moment of her forty-seven years was caused by a man almost young enough to be her child. Her old-fashioned upbringing kicked in every time that thought

40

crossed her mind. She should probably go to church to-morrow and pray for salvation, but she was pretty sure that she would be struck by lightning the moment she stepped foot over the threshold.

Her mother predicted that without Henry's steadying influence she would turn into a Jezebel. Sure, she was twenty years late in her predication but she was probably up in heaven right now dancing in glee. Kellista heard her cellphone ringing just as she finished cleaning the bath-room. Pulling her cleaning gloves off she picked up her phone to see who was calling.

"Oh great, just who I don't need." She muttered, seeing Henry's number pop up. The last thing she needed was to talk to her ex-husband while thinking of the younger man who possessed the capability of making her eyes roll back into her head. She hit the reject button to send his call to voice mail. Henry would just have to go onto her to-do list for later on in the week. One judgmental voice in her head was all she could take right now.

Her cellphone rang again. This time it was her older sis-ter Caleigh's number. Voice mail, here is another one for you. That was probably a mistake. Sure, enough the next phone call was from her sister Cynthia. Voice mail, here comes Cynthia. She was given only a few minutes of re-prieve before her cellphone dinged indicating she received a text message.

She looked at the message.

Drama Queens.

"If you don't call me back I am on the next flight to Colorado to kick your ghetto booty. xoxo Cynthia"

The temptation to ignore the text message was strong, but she knew that Cynthia was not bluffing. Knowing her she would probably go as far as to charter a private jet if she was feeling on a mission.

"Yes, Cynthia." she dusted her tv while dialing her sister.

"Hello, dahling, I am glad you could take the time out of your busy schedule to talk to me."

Let the eye rolling begin.

"Hold on a second while I get Caleigh on the line." Kellista listened to the silence as she waited for her sisters to come back.

"Okay you there dahling?" cue the southern belle. "Hey Kell, what's up?"

"Hiya. I am good. Why did you call this family meeting?" she asked hoping to point out the ridiculousness of this phone call.

"This is not a family meeting, we just want to know how your night was, dahling."

"Fine, just fine." she gave a nice noncommittal answer.

"Who did you do?" Busted by the blunt force.

"What makes you think that I did anyone?" she crossed her fingers hoping that she sounded innocent enough not for them to question her further. She forgot that her older sisters were bulldogs.

"Oh girlie, don't try that innocent act on us. It didn't work when you were younger and it is not going to work now."

"I have no idea what you are talking about?" Alright this has gone beyond just a delaying technique it, now branched into fun.

"Little girl you are bucking for a…." Caleigh went off like Kellista knew she would.

She heard Cynthia sigh at our antics, "Cal. Why do you fall for her trick to distract you all the time?" Kellista couldn't help the giggles.

Conversation like this just reminded her of the fun of

growing up with them. She was always grateful they were close, even to this day.

"Stop it Kell. Just tell us how your night went."

No more stalling. I was time to confess her shame to her sisters. It didn't matter that she was forty-seven years old in their eyes she remained the little girl that used to follow them around, bugging the heck out of them.

"Imetaguywhoisthirty-twoyearsoldwhiteandwehadsex-onhisdesk." she hoped if she spoke fast enough they would not catch everything.

"What?" Cynthia shouted.

"Holy shit!" yelled Caleigh. Then the twin speak begins.

"Well when you cut…" Cynthia started.

"loose, you really cut loose." Caleigh finished.

"Younger man!"

"White."

"Sex on the Desk? Is that a new drink?"

"I didn't know…."

"that you had it in you."

"When do you see him again?"

"Or was this a one-night stand?" she didn't know which question she should answer first. She didn't even know if they expected an answer.

"Well." They both demanded in unison.

"I can't see him again." she groaned, "Didn't you hear the part where I said he was thirty-two?"

"So?" the twin speak again.

"So? So?" she was incredulous, "You know what mom would say if she found out I was dating a younger man. Especially one who is only five years older than Jeremy?"

"Honey I hate to be the one to break it to you," Cynthia was using the voice she reserved for her especially slow students, "but mom is dead." Like Kellista didn't know their mother passed on from cancer years ago.

"And you are not." Caleigh continued. "One marriage dictated by our mother is plenty. Isn't it time for you to start living your life for yourself and doing what you want not what is expected?" Older sisters could be wise. Even she had to admit they had a point.

"Don't let a guy you're into slip away because you are hung up on an archaic social norm." Cynthia continued.

"I didn't say I was into him." she denied.

"Dahling, you fucked him in public on a desk." Cynthia pointed out the obvious.

"It wasn't in public, it was in his office." she mumbled.

"Technicality." Both Cynthia and Caleigh stated.

"Jinx." The both shouted.

"Goodbye." she told them as they started their weird twin ritual and hung up the phone.

But they did give her something to think about. Could she let go of her upbringing enough to give Jericho a chance? Did he even want a chance?

She didn't know. Perhaps she would have to wait and see.

CHAPTER SEVEN

KELLISTA FINALLY FINISHED cleaning her house, but continued dodging phone calls from her son and her ex-husband. They were being persistent, but Kellista was being just as stubborn. She bit into an apple as she sat at her dining room table looking at a catalogue. She really needed to get new curtains for her living room, but couldn't decide on the style that she wanted.

Interrupting her focus, she had to get up as her doorbell ranged. Strange, nobody visited her on the weekends. She didn't have many friends other than April and Nancy, still be relatively new in Colorado Springs. Her sons would not make the trip from Denver to see her without ensuring that she was home first.

Curiosity got ahold of her when she looked through the peephole to see deputies from the El Paso County Sheriff department on her doorsteps.

She cracked the door open enough to speak to them without alerting them to the fact that she was home alone. Some habits where hard to kick from growing up in Denver.

"Officers."

"Ma'am." The one standing on her porch tipped his hat at her while the one standing a little behind him and to the side just nodded his head in acknowledgement. "We are trying to locate a Kellista Anthony."

Kellista was startled to find that they were looking for her, stepping out from behind her door she opened it wider.

"I am Kellista Anthony."

"Ma'am you are under arrest for assault and battery stemming from a bar fight last night. Please come with us." The sheriff deputy reached out and cuffed Kellista before escorting her to the Sheriff's car parked behind her own vehicle.

Kellista was in shock. She'd never been arrested before. She watched as the second sheriff deputy closed her front door, carrying her purse with him as he got into the car.

Well fuck. *'What else could happen this weekend?'* she thought as they drove away from her house.

CHAPTER EIGHT

JERICHO TURNED ON his television in his kitchen to catch the news taking a break from Operation get Kellista. He stuck his head in the fridge listening to the news absently looking at the selection of food his chef left him for over the weekend. He pulled his head out of the fridge at the mention of Club Envy on the news.

Last night lead singer Delicious, of the Sex Kittens, was attacked while partying at the elite Club Envy. Sources close to the singer says that a woman came out of nowhere claiming to be in a relationship with Jericho Ryder, the owner of Club Envy, and Delicious's fiancé. We haven't been able to get in touch with Mr. Ryder, but a spokesperson for Delicious says that she is in the hospital for observation, but is expected to make a full recovery. Police have a suspect in custody. The male newscaster reported.

"Oh, Jim how awful!" the female newscaster sympathized.

Jericho stood in front of his open refrigerator, mouth hanging open at the news. His cellphone started ringing and he groaned at the sight of his mother's number.

"Hello." he answered bracing himself for the tirade that he knew was coming.

"You are engaged to that two-bit, no singing, THOT-box?!" the bellow came through his cellphone. A small smile flitted across his face at his mother's use of slang. "THOT-box" he was going to have to speak to his younger brothers about teaching their mother slang. He wonders if they explained to her that it stood for That Hoe Over There or did they just let her use it willy-nilly?

"No, mother the news made a mistake." He explained, "I actually met a very nice lady last night."

"Really?" she stopped mid-tirade. "It's not this Deli-cious wench?" from new school to old school. That was his mother.

Flexible.

"No mother, she is a little older than me, but she is, I think, everything that I could desire in a woman." Jericho would never be anything but honest with his mother. They had been through too much together for him to be any-thing, but honest. "Mom, I would love to continue this conversation at a later date, but I have a feeling that I need to fix things with her after this news."

"Okay dear, call me when you get a chance. I love you."

"I love you too Mom." Jericho hung up his phone and shoved it back into his pocket. He grabbed his coat and car keys and headed to the garage.

He reviewed the security tapes of the altercation be-tween Delicious and Kellista last night after the ambulance left with Delicious to the local trauma center. The tape clearly showed Delicious stopping Kellista and preventing her from moving. It also showed Delicious throwing the first punch and Kellista defending herself.

Kellista's reflexes were impressive. He would remember not to piss her off.

The video was very informative. Jericho was a bit surprised at her strength, but impressed. He wanted to find her and let her know that what Delicious said was untrue, and get to know the feisty red head on a more personal note, perhaps she too had felt the spark. The thought spurred him into action, to get to know her, first he had to rescue her from Delicious's vindictiveness.

He connected his phone to the Bluetooth receiver before pulling out of his garage. "Dial Judge Daly." he spoke aloud to his phone. Time to go rescue his woman.

CHAPTER NINE

"KELLISTA ANTHONY." KELLISTA looked up from her conversation with the two women sitting next to her in the holding cell. They were discussing the proper information to put on a resume to attract the attention of human resource managers.

"Call me when you get out and I will help you set up your resume. Your years of prostitution can be declared as working in the service industry." She told the ladies as they were taking notes. Standing up she headed towards the front of the cell where the sheriff deputy waited.

"Yes." Kellista confirmed her identity.

"You have been released on bail." the deputy stated, "You have friends in high places." The deputy continued as he closed the cell door once she left it.

"Why?" Kellista was confused by the statement. Nancy and April were her only friends, both left this morning to spend the rest of the weekend in New Mexico at a spa.

"Arraignments and the posting of bail don't occur until Monday down at the county court, but your orders for bail came through today. Congratulations Mrs. Anthony you are the only person to be arrested today and leave today."

"Thanks, I think." she replied, even more confused. She didn't know anybody with that kind of pull. While following the sheriff deputy that lead her over to where she could sign for her things before being released, she tried to think who it could be.

She walked into the lobby of the Criminal Justice Center.

She stopped cold when she saw Jericho standing in the lobby. "You!" she shouted marching over to where he stood looking at something on his cellphone. She ignored how good he looked with his black hair mussed. He was wearing ass hugging jeans worn only as a favorite pair of jeans could be. A black t-shirt hugged his shoulders and chest. He looked good enough to eat. Kellista's pussy agreed as it soaked her panties at the sight of him.

Jericho moved towards her as she glared at him anger evident. His stride ate up the distance between them. He captured the fist that she was in the process of drawing back and used her momentum to sweep her up into his arms and kissing her fiercely. His mouth devoured hers. His tongue pushing past her lips to dominating her.

Kellista couldn't stop the moan that escaped her nor could she keep her hands from reaching up to claim their place in his hair. Tugging his head closer to her so that their kiss could be deepened.

They broke apart at the sound of a discrete cough behind them. Kellista opened her eyes, blinking several times to clear the haze induced by Jericho's kiss. Standing next to them was a tall slender brunette dressed in a pantsuit holding a briefcase.

"Mrs. Anthony," she smiled warmly at Kellista, "I am Jessica Wield, your attorney."

"I don't have an attorney." She stated confused as she unwrapped her arms from around Jericho. She should probably be thankful that he kept her from committing violence while on camera in the lobby of CJC, but she didn't want to. It was his fault that she was there in the first place. After all, he was a stupidly hot man! She stepped away from him only for him to reach out and pull her up against his also stupidly hot body. If he continued to look at her with those stupidly hot blue eyes she would not be responsible for attacking all of his stupidly hot everything.

"I was hired by Mr. Ryder to represent you." She pulled some papers from her briefcase. "I just need you to sign here and here." she indicated with a pen, "It is giving me permission to represent you in this matter against Miss Stacie Caughman and any future actions dealing with her."

"Who is Stacie Caughman?" she asked as she signed where the attorney indicated.

"Delicious." Jericho spoke for the first time.

"Oh. Why are you here getting me out of jail instead of with your Barbie doll dumb girlfriend?" Kellista didn't know how to respond nicely, after all he had made her a homewrecker. Her initial anger and shock at seeing Jericho still existed.

"She is not my girlfriend." He stated firmly.

"Are you sure she knows that?" she stated just as firmly as he did.

"There is nothing going on between me and Delicious. I treat her no differently than I treat the other women in my club."

"Oh, so I am not the only one that got your desk treatment?" her eyebrow shot up at that news that there were more victims of his club routine.

"Never." The emphatic statement burst forcibly out of

his mouth, the anger at her insinuation was easy for everyone to hear. "I have a strict policy not to fuck with the women in my club. It's bad for business. You made that policy go straight out the window." He gathered her up into his arms to convince her how serious he was, only to be interrupted again.

"Mr. Ryder arranged for you to get out of jail." Jessica stated as she placed the papers back into her briefcase. "Now don't you worry about anything, Mrs. Anthony, I will handle it from here on out. It was a pleasure to meet you." She held out her hand and Kellista shook it.

Jessica picked up her briefcase. "I will be in touch Mr. Ryder." She turned to walk out of CJC. She paused, hesitating a moment before leaving them turning back to Kellista. "Mrs. Anthony, for the record, Mr Ryder has not nor ever been in a relationship with Ms. Caughman." She then continued on her way.

Kellista turned towards Jericho. "I can't afford a lawyer." She informed him.

He ignored her instead taking off his jacket and wrapping it around her shoulders, there was a slight chill in the air from an approaching rainstorm. It was too big on her, but he liked the sight of her wearing something that belonging to him. He tucked her into his side as they left the building. Daylight had long since gone since Kellista's arrival, the temperatures dropping with the advancement of night. He opened the car door for her.

Kellista stopped. Pausing to stare at the car they were about to get into.

"This is your car?" she asked in disbelief.

Jericho shrugged. "Yep, bought and paid for." He was used to that reaction. After all it was not often that someone his age could afford such an expensive car. Gently he helped her into the passenger seat before going around to the driver's side.

Kellista didn't know much about owning a nightclub, but it must be a lucrative business since she was sitting in the front seat of a Porsche Cayman S that was sitting on twenty-inch sports techno rims.

Jericho got into the car and started it up. From the sound of it, Kellista could clearly hear the three points four engine that could pull an impressive three hundred and twenty-five horsepower. Her middle son would be green with envy. This was his dream car and he would die when she told him that not only she seen it, but she rode in it. Nothing drives a gearhead crazier than knowing that their mother got to experience their dream before them.

Kellista had to wonder, how Jericho could afford such an expensive car? She almost bit her tongue in half to prevent herself from asking. His finances were not any of her business.

"What is your address, darling?" Jericho asked her.

She looked at him in surprise, "You don't know it?"

He grinned at her as he put the car in gear. "Actually, I do, but I didn't want to freak you out by admitting it." He turned in the direction of her home.

"Stalker much?" she mumbled under her breath nervous sitting in his car.

Jericho didn't say anything as he drove to her house. When he pulled to a stop in her driveway Kellista jumped out of the car.

"Uh thanks for coming to get me. I will see you later, bye." She said in a rush hoping that he got the hint not to get out of the car. Once she closed the door, she rushed to her front door. Thank goodness, the sheriff deputy grabbed her house keys before arresting her. She would have to write a letter to the Sheriff commending his staff. Another thing to add to her to do list.

She heard the car door slamming behind her and Jericho's footsteps as he strode up her walkway. She burst into her house and turning to close the door on him. He put his hand out to stop her.

"We need to talk." he quietly stated, easily keeping the door from closing.

Releasing a sigh, she opened the door wide enough to letting him pass into her house. He did bail her out of jail, so she wasn't going to avoid this discussion no matter how desperately she wanted to.

CHAPTER TEN

JERICHO LOOKED AROUND Kellista's house, taking it all in. It was cute. Big enough for just one person. He liked that. It meant that there was not a serious man in Kellista's life. No bodies for him to get rid of. That simplified things tremendously.

He looked at an intricately sewn quilt in the glass frame hanging on the wall.

Kellista saw him looking at it and move to stand in front of it. "This has been in my family for generations." she explained. "It was rumored to help slaves find their way to freedom with the Underground Railroad." She reached out and gently touched the glass.

"It is beautiful." Jericho stated watching Kellista study the quilt.

Kellista shook her head as if waking up. Then she took a deep breath before finally turning towards Jericho. "Have a seat." she gestured to the living room, "Are you hungry? I can cook you something. Do you need a drink?" she babbled nervously.

Jericho shook his head, "No, I'm fine." He sat down on the sofa and patted the spot next to him, gently asking her to sit next to him. He thought she was going to ignore him as she shrugged out of his jacket walking over to a chair. Instead, she draped his jacket over the chair before taking the seat next to him.

As soon as she sat down, he pulled her next to him, Jericho wrapped his arms around her. At first, she was stiff, but after a few minutes of fighting it he felt her relax against him.

"So, you want to explain to me how I ended up in jail?" she asked after a few minutes of them sitting their quietly.

He could feel her hand resting on him. He wondered if she realized that she was petting him. He kept quiet about it in case she decided to stop.

"Delicious has been chasing me for months now. Her career is not going as well as she wants and so she decided that it would be easier to be a MRS instead of a singer. Unfortunately for me I am the poor sap that she has decided that could give her the lifestyle that she wants." He let out a sigh.

"She been persistent. The only thing that she has been unable to do is penetrate the security of my house. Those who know the location of my house have signed a nondisclosure agreement with a penalty so steep that their great-great-great-great grandchildren would still be paying it off." He snuggled Kellista close to him. He took great pleasure in the scent of her hair. It reminded him of freshly baked sugar cookies.

"The fight with you last night was a new tactic. I guess she figures she could scare off the competition. That didn't work with you so she resorted to the story of you attacking her and having you arrested. Since it is my fault that you are in this situation I will pay for your lawyer."

Kellista sat up and looked at him shocked. "I am not competition." she stated.

He gathered her back into his arms against minimum resistance. "No, your right you're not competition. You're the winner."

Her head popped up at that statement, "What?" Jericho would have laughed at the panic in her eyes if his future didn't depend on calming her down and keeping her from running from him figuratively if not literally.

He sat up slowly from his slouched position, turning so he could look her in the eye. "I know we just met, but I also know that we shared a spark, without a doubt. Should you not be opposed, I would like to see where that spark goes." Cupping her cheek, he brought her face closer for his lips to reach her. When he eliminated the distance, he kissed her gently, then continuing on to each eyelid when they fluttered closed at his soft kiss.

"We can start over and take it slow, get to know each other until you come to terms with our relationship, but have no doubt Kellista Anthony in the end you will be mine." He kissed her again gently on her lips before he stood up striding out of her home.

Kellista followed him to the door and watched him walk to his car. He waved to her before he backed out of her driveway.

Kellista closed and locked her front door before slumping against it.

'What the hell did I just get myself into?' She thought as she touched her still tingling mouth.

CHAPTER ELEVEN

MONDAY MORNING, SHE walked into work with her professional face on. Kellista manage to dodge April and Nancy's phone calls all weekend, but she knew that luxury would now be over. She could only deal with one set of sisters at a time and the biological ones got a hold of her first. Pile on the drama of being arrested and Jericho's declaration and she was stretched to the max.

She knew safety would be gone once she was within walking range. No sooner she entered her office when April came barging in with a cup of coffee in her hand. She handed it to Kellista.

"Okay girl, spill it," she demanded, "and I don't mean the coffee."

Plausible deniability is what she was going for right now. Looking April dead in the eye, "I have no idea what are you talking about." She shifted her gaze away, instead turning on her computer to start her work day. This wouldn't work on her older sisters, but maybe it would work on April.

"Oh, hell no!" April said, "You are not getting off that

easy. You disappeared on us Friday night only to turn up looking like you just got the life fucked out of you. I have waited all weekend to find out what happened!" Damn April was just as tough to dodge as Cynthia or Caleigh.

She wasn't going to be able to get rid of her without some sort of explanation. Maybe she could even help her. She had been debating the advice that her older sisters gave her, to take a chance on Jericho, all weekend. It had gotten her nowhere. As a single woman around the same age as her, April would understand her concern about dating a younger man and could probably give her solid advice. Decision made, she sat down heavily in her chair. "I am a cradle robber." she moaned at the words spoken out loud. It sounded even worse when voiced.

Laughter was not the reaction she expected to get from April, but laughter is what she got. "Cradle robber." she hooted.

"Really?" she looked at her shocked and annoyed. This just caused April to hoot even louder. "April, we are in a place of business. Control yourself." If all else fails, fall back on training.

After a few hiccups and a snort, April stopped laughing. "Why do you think you are a cradle robber?"

"You do realize that Jericho is only a few years older than my oldest son?" she informed her.

"And…."

"What do you mean and?" She was totally not helping her, Kellista thought.

"Just what I said. And. So, he is a few years younger than you. This is not the Victorian Era and there is nothing wrong with you dating a younger man. I thought you would have more problems with him being white rather than his age. Especially since you grew up with strict black parents." She stated.

She just stared at April in shock. Though, now that she thought about it, she realized that his color didn't matter. She was more hung up on his age.

"No, I don't care about him being white. Skin color is the result of natural selection and nobody can help the color they were born with." A lot of people have hang ups about skin tone, but it was not something she worried about in her lifetime and it was not something she was prepared to start worrying about now.

"Well then. You have played by the rules and what did that get you? Maybe it is time that you colored outside the lines and take a risk. Throw away the rules." She walked out of Kellista's office door leaving her to think about what she said.

Her comment followed Kellista throughout the day. She tried to concentrate on her job, but today was one of the days that she did not give her employers her all.

Why was she obsessing over this guy? Her mind flipped back and forth between Jericho's statement and April's.

She returned from lunch only to be stopped by the front desk lady before reaching her office.

"Oh Mrs. Anthony," she called out as Kellista passed, "this gentleman has been waiting on you." She gestured to the guy sitting in one of the lobby chairs sporting the uniform of the local florist. He stood up as she approached him.

"Can I help you sir?"

"Mrs. Anthony?" he inquired. At her nod, he handed her a clipboard. "Please sign here."

After signing where he indicated he handed her a beautifully potted lily and an envelope. She was surprised. These were the first flowers she had ever received. Kellista opened the note and read it quickly.

"I am to wait until you give an answer." the delivery guy said as she read the message. She looked up from the letter.

"Tell him I said Thank you, but no Thank you." She took the potted plant into her office and quietly shut the door, resisting the urge to slam it.

Looking over the message again.

My darling Kellista, being with you this weekend was something that I have never experienced before. It truly changed my life. I thought it would be best to give you a couple of days to think about it before I contacted you, but all I could do yesterday was think about you in my arms wishing for that moment again. I know I said that I would give you time, but I did not realize how long the day was without you. Will you please have dinner with me tonight so that we may discuss our future together. ~Jericho

She couldn't stop her heart from beating faster. Her body had instantly responded to seeing his name, it shocked her how her body would gladly do anything that Jericho suggested. Even her heart sided with her body on this one. But her mind was not so fickle, it remembered the pain of Henry's defection. Her mind refused to let her body or her heart speak for her again. She was not some young thing to be enamored with the idea of love at first sight, no matter the passion they shared.

There was a knock on her door.

Back to work.

"Come in." she called out. The door opened to reveal the delivery guy.

"Excuse me ma'am. I was instructed that in the event that your answer was no I was to give you this envelope." He handed her another envelope before closing the door. She could see through the window of the door that he finally truly left.

She opened this one to read what was written inside.

Roses are Red.
Lilies are cool.
I tried sweet and mushy
But your too stubborn (I know that totally ruins the rhyme).
Roses are Red
Lilies are still cool.
Don't take me for a fool.
Who's going to give up on you.

She couldn't stop herself from smiling at the bad poetry. She knew she should run for the hills, after all it was so sudden. Her mind kept screaming for her to get far away from Jericho before he broke her fragile heart again. She couldn't be strong a second time.

She kept thinking about what April said earlier.

Could she color outside of the lines?

Her heart shouted "Yes!" louder than her mind shouted "No".

Chapter Twelve

Jericho wasn't at all surprised when the florist returned the answer of "No." Kellista wasn't going to make things easy, but he had a feeling that she was worth it in the end. This was just the start of his campaign to win her heart. He thought the whole arrest episode would have thrown a wrench into his plan, but her response to his kiss at CJC and the fact that she didn't protest him hiring her an attorney were points in his favor.

He opened his phone and viewed the text message she had sent him.

Roses are red.
Violets are blue.
You are nutty as hell.
If you think I am going to date you.

He laughed out loud as he reread her text. No, the arrest wasn't the problem. It was the media that was at the root of all his problems.

He read his response to her.

Some nuts are round.
Some nuts have shells
My nuts are blue
Please can I date you?

He continued to deal with the media frenzy caused by Delicious's announcement of their engagement on the news and the slanderous story that she was putting out about her attacker. He paid a publicist to handle the media. She released a statement about Delicious being mistaken about their relationship due to her injury.

It was in his favor that the news hadn't released Kellista's name and so only those who seen the altercation knew of her involvement. The only reason the sheriff deputies had been able to find her is that Malcolm provided the information. He was under orders to cooperate with law enforcement and provided her name to them when they came to question the staff on that Saturday morning.

Jericho had seen the note that Malcolm made in his daily report. The report was waiting for him on the following Monday when he came to the club. Malcolm didn't know that Kellista was a bit more than a regular club goer to Jericho. He only thought of her as another guest otherwise he would have informed Jericho of the sheriff's deputies visit. Jericho didn't like finding out about Kellista's arrest on the news. Malcolm now had a new awareness of Kellista status in Jericho's life and that all information pertaining to anything happening to her while in Club Envy was to be reported to Jericho immediately. This would ensure he could deal with any similar situations. Not that he anticipated future problems.

All of the publicity only served to swell the crowds at Club Envy. It was great for business, but so far in the week it served to suck out the chances for his new potential love life. Each new media story caused Kellista to dig in her heels about going out with him. Day after day he received her rejections. How could he make progress with her if she refused to see him?

Every delivery, except for the Lily, was returned to him. The returns were accompanied by a text from her asking him to stop sending the gifts.

He in return would ask her out via text.

She would refuse.

He would refuse to stop sending gifts. He even went so far as to not only send the original gift back to her, but to include similar gift to the two women, Nancy and April.

This underhanded move won him allies.

His phone dinged.

Blue balls

Red balls.

Purple balls too.

No way in heck am I dating you.

He immediately responded.

Is that a challenge?

He didn't have to wait long for a response.

I have no recollection of what you are talking about?

Her humorous approach to each response gave Jericho a glimpse of her playful side. It became a game between them to see who could write the wackiest message. A game that he hoped ended in her consenting to go on a date with him.

Though, he was having fun teasing Kellista through text

messages. By the end of the week, he was beginning to feel frustrated. The delivery guy was seeing more of her then he was. Jericho never thought this moment would come in his life. He was desperate. It was time for him to pull out the big guns.

It was to the point where he couldn't get any work done at his desk. All he did was remember how beautiful she looked spread out on his desk. His cock would grow hard at the fantasies of her being spread out on his desk with him sitting in his office chair started to become commonplace instead of work.

He rolled his chair in between her beautiful thighs. Perfectly positioned for him to gently spread them apart so he could have an unobstructed view of her neatly trimmed pussy. He began rubbing his cheek against the inside of her thighs, knowing his five o'clock shadow would redden her skin. Marking her as his. The taste of her on his tongue as it dipped between her lower lips was beyond his imagination. Running his tongue up her slit dripping with her wetness as his mouth closed over her clit. Sucking the responsive nub into his mouth he held her as she was writhing on his desk. Her hands burrowed in his hair pulling his head closer as her body arched up to meet his mouth. Moaning loudly as she demanded that he suck her harder.

"Hello?" answering his ringing phone, he absently glanced at the clock. The time abruptly ending his fantasy. His delivery should have been made. Almost a full week passed since he heard Kellista's voice. All their communication took place over text messages. So it came as a surprise when the sound of her voice echoed through the phone. His expression of shock quickly turned into a sly grin.

Success.

"You evil, evil, EVIL man!" she shouted through the phone.

"What?" Jericho could play the innocent role even

though he knew she was right. He was evil. Hey, all was fair in love and war. Despite what people may have thought this was war. A war for love. He settled comfortably in his office chair preparing to enjoy this phone conversation.

"Chocolate. You sent me chocolate. How cliché." Ahhhh, he thought. She was going to attack the act and not the gift. '*I bet this is gift won't be returned either.*' He thought smugly.

"You have got to stop wasting your money on sending me these expensive gifts!" she sounded exasperated. "I'm sure you have bills to pay and you don't need to waste your money on me."

His cock hardened at the sound of her whiskey-smooth voice. "I am glad you are enjoying my gifts. I too have enjoyed your responses to my asking you out." He chuckled softly.

"Don't worry about my bills. They are getting paid and you can still enjoy the chocolate." He could almost see the steam coming out of her ears at that statement.

"I'm allergic to chocolate." he could tell by the sound of her voice that she was lying.

"That is not what a little birdie told me." Kellista was a true chocolate connoisseur. He knew there was no way that she was going to give away the expensive Ecuadorian To'ak chocolate. Only a few shops in the U.S. carried it. He special ordered the chocolate from a store in Los Angeles, Kellista was worth the effort.

"So, darling, are you wearing any underwear?" he really wanted to know, and catch her off guard. It wouldn't have mattered if she was wearing any or not nothing would stop him from getting between those thighs again. Something his fantasy proved needed to happen sooner rather than later.

"Wouldn't you like to know." he wasn't expecting the

teasing Kellista from the way the phone conversation started. He loved it.

"Yes, yes I do want to know."

"Well too bad because that is not going to happen. Are you going to stop wasting your money on these gifts?" she asked shifting back to her earlier tone.

"Are you ready to go out to dinner with me?"

"No."

"Then the gifts continue. After all I don't want you to forget about me and how else can I stay on your mind if you won't see me?"

He heard her sigh through the phone. Victory was close.

"Fine, if I have dinner with you will you stop sending me the gifts?"

He sat up from his reclined position. "Tonight?"

"Yes. I will have dinner with you tonight." He pounded his fist on his desk. Finally, progress.

"I will send a car to pick you up at work." He told her before she could change her mind. He was already planning the dinner, what to wear, where to go... It would be perfect.

"Just let me know where to meet you at."

"Now darling, how are you going to meet me when your car is in the shop?" he asked innocently.

"Are you spying on me?" she demanded through the phone.

"No. A little birdie told me."

Kellista sighed in disgust. "A little birdie with a big fucking mouth. I am going to kill April."

"Maybe. Maybe not. But haven't you already spent enough time in jail? Do you really want to go back?" he teased her hoping to distract her. He needed his allies when it came to her.

"Yeah, your right. But I did have some interesting conversation. Did you know that I could charge up to fifty bucks for a decent blow job?" She said it so casually that it took him a minute to realize the words had even crossed her lips.

He groaned into the phone at the thought of her lips wrapped around his cock. Great. Just what he needed. Even more of a boner than he could cause on his own. That was playing dirty.

"Darling, I would pay you way more to have your mouth on my cock."

"Then it is a good thing that I am not for sell." she shot back.

"That is okay. Things are more valuable when you earn them instead of buying them. You cherish them more and I am definitely going to cherish you." he said smoothly.

"Hold up!" he smiled at the attitude that was coming through the phone. He sat back ready to enjoy the ride. "I have made it this far in life without you looking out for me and the last thing that I need is a child trying to protect me."

"A child?" he asked. He couldn't resist getting her hotter. "It was not a child causing you to moan and scream my name." Just the thought of how she looked displayed on his desk brought back his earlier fantasy.

"Oh no you didn't!" he could picture the blush creeping up her face as he reminded of her of their night together.

"Well, darling, I have to go. I will see you tonight." he hung up quickly before she could cancel. He pulled out his cellphone and texted his chef to prepare a special meal. Then he notified his housekeeper that he would be having a guest over tonight, but the staff wouldn't be needed.

Then it hit him. He genuinely wanted Kellista to like his

house. Jericho cared deeply about his privacy, thus the non-disclosure agreements, but he was willing to bring her, who he had just met, into his domain. If she didn't like his home, he had a feeling he would have no troubles making a change to something she did like. He was willing to turn his life upside-down for a woman. Surprisingly, the thought didn't make him want to run for the hills. This re-action never happened before when other women made it clear that they were more than willing for a permanent ar-rangement with him. The thought of long-term with Kel-lista didn't make him break out in hives. Kellista quickly became important to him. He just had to show her how important.

CHAPTER THIRTEEN

KELLISTA COULDN'T BELIEVE that little shit, the nerve to bring up their night together. At least by having dinner with him tonight she would stop the gifts from coming. Maybe it would also stop the constant thoughts that she continued to have of him. She'd just let him know that there could be no relationship between them.

All the media taking place since the night of her arrest was crazy. It wasn't something that she was prepared to deal with on a regular basis. Jericho associating with those who were newsworthy on a regular basis was mind blowing to her. If she did take a risk and date him it would be only a matter of time before the media found out about it and then how would society look upon her?

A woman of her age dating a man of his age?

Sure, that type of thing was seen as normal on the movie scene, but they were a far cry from any major movie studio. Colorado housed its own share of uptight bible thumpers.

She cringed at the mere thought of people's reactions.

Especially her sons. The two younger ones not so much as her oldest. Hypocrite thy name is Jeremy.

Double standard should have been his middle name instead of Edward.

No, she was not equipped to compete with the socialites that amassed in Jericho's sphere. Every time she thought that, she remembered his words. That there was no competition, she was the winner. Then she would remind herself, no, she couldn't give in to the hope that was warming her heart.

There definitely could not be a relationship between her and Jericho. She firmly told herself.

She smiled at thought of the gifts he sent. Someone had taught Jericho right. He didn't send her expensive jewelry or useless perfume.

No, he sent her expensive chocolate and expensive wine. He sent lunch to her office with enough to share with April and Nancy. Thoughtful gifts. Gifts from the heart.

Good manners dictated that she return the non-edible items. She couldn't accept presents from someone she was not in a relationship with. When she texted Jericho to tell him so, they ended up in a text war. It made her laugh at some of the crazy things he texted to her. Somehow, he always managed to ask her if she was wearing any underwear. She would always tease him with a response that left him guessing. Lord only knew what he would do if she answered truthfully. She wouldn't put it past him to show up on her doorstep to verify her answers. Kellista knew, without a doubt that she didn't have the willpower to turn him away. She wasn't even sure if her body would let her. She craved his touch more than she craved chocolate and chocolate was God.

He even sent dinner one night when she was working

late. How he knew she was working late that night was beyond her, but she figured either April or Nancy was spying for him. Perhaps even both were, who knew? He got points for being thoughtful though. She had sat at her desk with a goofy smile on her face.

It was nice having a man think about her. She was a strong woman, but once in a while it was nice to have someone to lean on. Her ex-husband Henry was always too busy building up his business to help her solve any of the problems at home. She was always left to come up with a solution on her own. It was tiring carrying the burden of a marriage and a family on her shoulders alone. Especially when your partner left all the worrying to you, but didn't mind reaping the benefits of you creating a safe home and a welcoming home life. Even though they didn't know each other long, she got the distinct feeling that Jericho wouldn't be that type of partner. He would help to carry the burden, making sure that the load was equal if not shouldering the whole burden himself. But that was not the type of partnership she would be satisfied with. It was equal partners or nothing at all.

She shook her head to clear those thoughts from her head. There was enough on her plate right now then to dream about a relationship that would never happen. She needed to figure out why someone slashed all of her tires. She came out of her house this morning to leave for work to find all of her tires were flat. She couldn't remember running over anything that would cause all of her tires to lose air. It was only after she called road side assistance and they examined her tires that they told her that they were deliberately slashed. It was at their insistence that she called the police, especially when they found that her cover for her gas tank pried off and sugar had been poured into her gas tank. That made it more than just vandalism, it was personal.

How they had even gotten to her locked gas tank was a mystery. She reported it to the police. They brushed it off as teenagers in her neighborhood playing pranks. Their only suggestion. Start parking her car in the garage.

Lord knows she couldn't afford another set of tires. The cost of her car being out of commission as the engine was being flushed was something she could do without also. It's not like she was raking in any alimony from Henry.

Even though Kellista's divorce lawyer determined that she was entitled to part of the company that Henry started she decided that she didn't want anything other than her half of their house. She didn't want any reason for continuing her contact with Henry. Her sons were enough of a reason. They were grown up, so it was not like she was going to hear from him that often. He did all the work to start that company, he could keep all of the rewards. The lawyer argued that the only reason Henry was able to dedicate so much time to his company is because she kept things together at home for him, that entitled her to some of the benefits of the company.

Finally, Kellista agreed to a stipulation, if he sold the company then she would receive half of the proceeds from the sale, satisfying her lawyer's need to draw blood and providing her with a potential nest egg. Meanwhile, she scaled back her lifestyle, but she was free of Henry and that was enough for her.

She was a firm believer in Karma. Henry would get his when he least expected it.

Looking down she realized that she doodled Jericho's name on the pad that she used for taking notes on.

She had to snap out of it. There is no future in having

these thoughts she told herself, though it was less firmly than a week ago when she first met him. Jericho managed to make her smile more in the past week than anyone else had been able to do in a long time. Who knew her life could change so much in less than a week?

When she talked to him on the phone she had no intention of agreeing to have dinner with him. She was truly surprised when she agreed. She just knew that she didn't feel as strongly about their age difference as when they first meet. She found herself thinking about him throughout the day and when she went home to her empty house, there was nothing to distract her from thoughts of him.

Once more, she was startled from her thoughts by a knock on her door. She looked up to see a delivery person. She reached out to sign the electronic pad. The woman turned away and left as soon as she handed Kellista the package. Not a word spoken between the two of them. She shrugged, guess not all delivery people were friendly.

Kellista set the box in the middle of her desk and grabbed a pair of scissors to open it. She cut part of it open when her computer alarm went off reminding her of a meeting. She dropped the scissor and grabbed the stack of papers she placed on her desk. She had forgotten that she was covering the new employee orientation for one of her human resource personnel who called in sick.

Kellista rushed out of her office heading towards the conference room. She met up with the other two human resource employees that were going to assist her. There was fairly large group of new employees starting.

"Ah dang, I forget the folders. Hey Rob can you go grab that box of folders off of my desk for me please." Thoughts of Jericho were making her more absent-minded.

Kellista went to work setting up the conference room

with Crystal. They were almost done before she realized that Rob hadn't returned with the folders.

"What the heck is taking Rob so long?"

Crystal gave her an amused look. "You haven't been here long enough to know that Rob has a thing for Maria and he has to go right past her desk to get to your office. That is twice the opportunity to stare at her in stupefaction."

Kellista rolled her eyes. Men. Easily distracted.

"I will go get him!" Crystal said as she headed out the door.

Kellista was finishing up with the pens when she heard a loud scream. She rushed out of the conference room in the direction it came from. She ended up at her office door to find Crystal screaming hysterically and a crowded gathering around, clamoring to see.

"What?" she asked grabbing ahold of Crystal.

All Crystal could do was point into Kellista's office as she buried her face into Kellista's shoulder.

Kellista looked over the crying woman to see a pair of feet laying on her floor. She recognized the pants as the one that Rob was wearing earlier. She pushed Crystal aside to rushing in his direction. She was jerked to a halt by Crystal's death grip on her arm. She was going to have to find out what it was about that arm that made other women want to grab it.

"Don't go in there!" Crystal cried pulling her back towards the door.

"But we have to help Rob." Kellista didn't understand why Crystal was stopping her. She turned to remove Crystal's hand from her arm when she heard a rattle, like a baby rattle.

She turned back to her office where the sound was coming from. She looked around trying to locate the source. Then she saw the second package delivery sitting on its side. Rob must have knocked it off her desk when he picked up the folders, she thought absently continuing to look around.

The rattling noise echoed around once more.

From behind her desk slithered several snakes. The snakes varied in color from green to light brown. One of the snakes raised up in the air, tongue flickering out of its mouth as if tasting the air. Its yellow underbelly visible. Tail rattling in warning.

"OH Shit!" Kellista exclaimed. She stepped back out of her office and slammed the door. The sounds of sirens could be heard. The fire alarm sounded. People started to evacuate the building. Kellista followed behind Crystal. Too stunned to do anything else.

"Why the fuck are their snakes in my office?"

CHAPTER FOURTEEN

KELLISTA SAT IN the front seat of Crystal's car. They retreated to her car when the October wind picked up making it too cold to stand outside without a coat. They were lucky that Crystal always carried her car keys in her pants pocket. It wouldn't have done them any good if the situation were reversed, her car was at the shop.

Neither one of them carried their cellphones on them. It was human resource policy: no cellphone usage during new employee orientation.

It was believed to set the right tone for the employees. That they were there to work. Not to Candy Crush or Facebook their way through the day.

The police were waiting to question them about what had taken place. Someone from both Colorado Springs Police Department and the El Paso County Sheriff Department came by and asked them not to leave the premises.

Animal control cleared the snakes from the building. Crystal finally stopped crying when they saw Rob being wheeled out on a gurney and loaded into an ambulance.

They received news that the local trauma center was on standby with anti-venom for the snake bites. Rob was lucky that he'd been bitten by a common Prairie Rattlesnake. It could be found throughout Colorado. The unseasonably warm weather of the past few weeks explained why they were still around. It was still a week before Halloween, when the cold winter made itself known in Colorado in the form of a snowstorm for the trick-or-treaters. The unanswered question is why were they in her office and how did they get there?

They were sitting in Crystal's car for a little while running the heater when someone tapped Kellista's window. Kellista looked up to see both a deputy sheriff and a Springs police officer at the window. She hit the button to let the window down.

The police officer spoke, "Ma'am. Ma'am" he nodded to both Crystal and her. "The building is in the jurisdiction of the Colorado Springs Police they will be handling the inquiry into what has happened here."

Kellista nodded her head as he spoke. "We are escorting everyone who work on your floor back into the building to collect their belongings. When you are ready ma'am I will escort you to your office where you may collect your purse and your coat but nothing else. Is that understood?" At Kellista's nod he opened the car door for her to step out into the cold wind. Winter was indeed just around the corner. She rushed behind him shivering as she crossed the parking lot into the building.

She continued to shiver once in the building. It was just as cold inside as it was outside. "They shut off the heat hoping it would fool the snakes into going into hibernation and drive them." The officer must have read her mind.

They rode the elevator up to her floor. She expected it

to be empty, but there was bustling of professionals in uniforms everywhere. The police officer gripped her by the elbow, guiding her towards her office. She stopped in her doorway. Unable to cross the threshold. She looked to where she seen Rob's legs sticking out from behind her desk, expecting to see them there, but knowing he had been removed.

She removed her keys from her pocket and picked the desk key out. She handed it to the officer. "My purse is in the bottom left drawer. It is the only one with a lock on it."

He handed her keys to a woman wearing gloves who went over to the desk and retrieved her purse. Her winter coat, or she should say Jericho's jacket was still thrown across the back of her office chair from where she placed it when she took it off this morning. She wasn't going to admit to him that she been wearing it every day. She loved how the jacket smelled just like him. It was big enough to engulf her and made her feel like she was surrounded by him. The woman officer grabbed it and brought it with her purse to Kellista.

Kellista slipped the jacket on aware of the officer watching her.

"Is this a *Johan* original?" he asked her.

"Excuse me?" she didn't understand the question.

"The jacket. It is from this year's *Johan's* Winter Collection." He looked at her expectantly, "You know. *Johan?* The hottest men's designer. He designs men clothing. He dresses NFL players, NHL players, rappers and some of the most up and coming stars." He talked as if talking about his favorite action actor or sports star, not a clothing designer. Kellista was saved from answering by ringing coming from her coat pocket. Saved by the bell, literally.

She looked at the screen and sighing in relief when she

saw it was Jericho. She didn't ask the officer if it was okay for her to answer it. Stepping away from him, turning her back to answer the call, giving an illusion of privacy where there was none.

"Hello."

"Hey, why haven't you been answering your text messages?" Jericho demanded.

"Hey Jericho." She breathed out unaware how her voice softened as she spoke to him, "There was an incident at my job and the building was evacuated."

"Are you, all right?"

"Where are you?"

"Stay right there I am coming to get you." The rapid-fire orders followed one after another.

She chuckled softly at his reaction. She knew he would go into alpha mode and she would deny it to anyone who asked, but she liked it.

"How can you come get me when you don't know where I am at?" She teased him.

"Well darling," he drawled, "what you don't know is that I lojacked your ass. I will always find you."

"Well don't rush down here. The police have to ask me some questions and they will not let you into the building." She informed him not wanting him to make a wasted trip.

"You just let me worry about the police. I will be there in a few minutes. Love you." Jericho told her before hanging up the phone.

Kellista gripped her phone tightly in her hands. Jericho's words went straight to her heart. It felt like it wanted to burst from her chest. She turned around to face the officer.

"Okay. Let's get this over with." She straightened her should allowing him to lead her away from her office.

Chapter Fifteen

KELLISTA LOOKED UP at the commotion at the door to see Jericho striding into the room. Her mouth dropped open at the sight of him. Not just because he was looking hotter than hell in the custom suit he was wearing, but surprised they allowed him to enter what the police termed an "active crime scene".

The whole atmosphere changed with his presence. The room seemed to be of adequate size before his arrival, but it shrunk, getting smaller once he entered it. All of the air seemed to have been sucked out of the room as a side effect.

Kellista and the officer had been joined by an older detective around Kellista's age who had taken over the questioning. His line of questioning was more direct then the other officer. Even Kellista was aware they were pulling a version of good cop, bad cop on her. She was not stupid. They didn't believe her when she told them she didn't know how the snakes got into her office. She did not send Rob in there on purpose to be bitten.

"Gentlemen." Jericho's deep voice sent shivers down her spine. Hearing it in person was different then hearing it across a phone line.

He stood there.

Tall.

Broad shoulders.

Looking absolutely delicious.

An air of authority surrounded him, causing the men in the room to give him deferential treatment. Where they were hard-edged and demanding with her, they subconsciously bowed to his dominance.

Detective Miller, the older officer, tried to reassert his dominance in the room.

"Who are you?"

"Who let you in?" He demanded.

From behind Jericho stepped Jessica Wield. Nobody noticed her presence in his shadow. She smoothly held out her hand to Detective Miller, "Detective, I am Jessica Wield, Mrs. Anthony's attorney. I am here to represent her interests as you question her."

"Then who are you?" Detective Miller jerked his chin in Jericho's direction as he shook Jessica's hand.

"This is Mr. Ryder. Mrs. Anthony fiancé. He is her for her support." Jessica answered his questions. She turned and pulled out a seat next to Kellista and indicated Jericho should sit there. Then she pulled out the chair on the other side of Kellista and sat in it herself. Once comfortable, she opened her briefcase pulling out a tablet and mini-recorder.

Kellista just sat in her seat stunned. A minute ago, it was her against the Colorado Springs Police Department. Just by entering the room Jericho changed the whole dynamics of the situation. That was the power of his personality. Jericho didn't sit down immediately. Instead he pulled Kellista up out of her seat. He shrugged out of the overcoat he was wearing unbuttoned over his suit and draped it around her shoulders; over the jacket of his she was already wearing. He helped her slide her arms into the overcoat before helping her sit back in her seat.

Kellista heard Officer Wilder, who escorted her to the room, mumble under his breath.

"Damn, he is wearing a *Johan* original overcoat and a custom-made suit. Who is this guy?"

Kellista looked at Jericho. The grey suit hugging his rugged body, highlighting his extreme level of fitness. The fit went beyond nice, it was obvious only he could wear the suit and deal with the consequences of being elevated to devastatingly handsome. He exuded an untouchable air of sophistication. The blue of his shirt made his already beautiful blue eyes sparkle. There was no mistaking Jericho for anything other than a wealthy sophisticated man who could afford the best.

There was no mistaking the pride filling Kellista.

This was her man.

CHAPTER SIXTEEN

REACHING OUT JERICHO clasped Kellista's hand in his. It was obvious to him the officers were not hearing what they wanted from Kellista. Detective Miller had assumed an antagonistic posture towards Kellista. Jericho wasn't even aware of what happened. Even if Kellista was guilty there was no way he was letting her go without a fight. Jessica Wield was going to earn her retainer fee.

Detective Miller looked at their clasped hands. "Ryder. Ryder." he repeated to himself.

"I was under the impression that you were married, Mrs. Anthony." he put extra emphasis on his statement.

"Mrs. Anthony is divorced." Jessica answered for Kellista. He saw Kellista's mouth drop open at this. She looked at him. He raised his eyebrow at her giving a small, gentle smile. Yeah, there were perks to having a lawyer.

"Officers why exactly are you questioning my client?" he watched Jessica in action. Many made the mistake of thinking the tall willowy brunette was weak as her frame suggested. They quickly learned how much they underestimated

85

her.

"*Mrs.* Anthony received a package earlier which resulted in the near death of one of her fellow employees. We take that kind of attack very seriously." Detective Miller turned his antagonism towards Jessica. Jericho was about to demand he change his tone when Jessica proved she could easily put the detective in his place.

"Let me get this correct, *officer.*" She put the same emphasis on his title as he put on the Mrs. "My client was the recipient of a package and you are questioning her like she is a suspect. Does anyone else see something wrong with this picture?" Jessica asked the question to the room at large, but didn't wait for a reply. "Did you stop to think that my client could have been the target of this attack, officer?"

"Well…" Jessica powered on before he could finish his statement.

"Are you basing your assumptions of the guilt on my client because of her skin color, *officer?*" Jessica was on a roll. She left the detective speechless.

"I think we are finished here officers." Jessica stood up and started packing her tablet and mini-recorder back into her briefcase. "If you have any further questions for Mrs. Anthony, please feel free to contact my office. In the meantime, I would suggest you try to find out who is trying to kill Mrs. Anthony or I will call for a departmental review." She handed all of the officers in the room a business card. She turned and gestured towards the door. Prior to them walking out the door Detective Miller spoke again. "Are you *the* Jericho Ryder?"

"Yes, he is." Jessica answered gesturing to the door again. It seemed the officers were not done with his questions. "I heard that you were engaged to a singer." Office Wilder snapped his fingers trying to recall a name. "What is her name? Delicious." Officer Wilder said triumphantly.

"That was a case of bad reporting," Jessica fielded the question, "as I stated before Mr. Ryder is engaged to Mrs. Anthony."

Kellista let Jericho lead her out of the room after her statement. Maybe she needed to check into why she was allowing herself to be led around like a trained monkey along with the whole grabby arm thing. The week just continued sliding into insanity.

Jericho ushered Kellista to the elevator. The ride down was quiet, everyone contemplated the events that just took place. In less than fifteen minutes Jericho and Jessica had Kellista out of what was without a doubt an uncomfortable questioning and on her way home. She didn't know anyone else who could have extracted her from the situation so efficiently. Definitely not Henry. He would probably be on the police's side.

Kellista slide into Jericho's car without a peep. What was the point in arguing? Her car was in the shop and she needed a ride home. "I hope you still plan to feed me dinner?" she asked him as her stomach rumbled loudly rivaling the growl of the Porsche.

"Of course, I am, darling." Jericho spoke for the first time. He reached out pulling her over the gear shift. His mouth covering her's kissing her as if it was his last kiss in the world. Kellista moaned as he plundered her mouth. She sat back dazed when he released her mouth. "Dinner is the first thing I am going to feed you." He said as he smoothly shifted into gear.

CHAPTER SEVENTEEN

KELLISTA WAS SURPRISED when they drove toward an exclusive neighborhood, she had anticipated a restaurant. Not all million-dollar homes were located in the Broadmoor. She knew. She did the research during her own house hunt.

She purchased her home in what the realtor termed a "revitalized area", but she was sure that was just an excuse to up the asking price. The neighborhood they were heading to was way out of her price range.

It was becoming more and more obvious that Jericho had money. Lots and lots of it by the looks of the houses they're passing. Kellista was jealous of these homes. The view of Pikes Peak was great. The lots also contained large amounts of space between neighbors. Privacy. Jericho pulled up to a closed gate inputting a code before proceeding up the driveway of a summer cottage. She blinked a couple of times looking at it.

It was beautiful.

It was huge.

It was Jericho's.

She didn't know much about Jericho beyond the fact that he owned Club Envy and he was younger than she was and he drove a kick ass car. He had wonderful taste in chocolate and he was the hottest fuck ever. Well, perhaps she did know more about him then she thought. Though she needed to find out some adult information about him.

This was her new mission. She disregarded her earlier thoughts of telling him they could not have a relationship. She knew the idea went out the window when Jessica claimed her as his fiancé. After all, she would only have done that with his permission. Even though she had only known him for a week she was surprisingly not totally opposed to the idea. For now, she could live with being his fiancé. She wasn't ready to tell her family that quite yet.

Jericho pulled up into the circular driveway. Kellista didn't attempt to open the door and get out of the car, she waited for him to come around and open the door for her. She thought his old-fashion manners was sweet. He acknowledged she was capable of getting out of the car unassisted, but it was his duty to make sure she was safe when in his presence He stepped aside to allow her entrance into his home.

As soon as he closed the door, he pulled her into his arms and kissed her deeply. She didn't even realize her eyes drifted closed at the touch of his lips.

"Hello, Darling." he said when he lifted his mouth from hers.

"Hello, Jericho." She pressed her mouth against his. She loved the taste of him.

The ringing of her cellphone broke the spell their mouths were weaving. She pulled back to answer only to have it stop ringing. Jericho lowered his mouth to continue their kissing when her phone started ringing once more. She looked down to see who was calling her. One of the few people she couldn't just ignore.

"Hello, Jeremy." she answered with resigned sigh. She was not in the mood to get into another argument with him. She had enough drama for the day.

Jericho looked questioning at her as she answered the phone.

She silently mouthed the words, "My son." at him. She concentrated on the call; Jericho guided her through his house. He took her work bag from her and place it on a side table. Then he proceeded to help her out of his over-coat and then his jacket which he hung up in the hall closet. He guided Kellista to the dining room and pulled out a chair for her to sit in before disappearing into the kitchen.

"Mother." Jeremy's formal way of talking drove her nuts.

"Son." she returned just as formally.

"I am calling to invite you to a parents' dinner with Janet and I. I am informing you early to ensure that you have plenty of warning so that you don't have a scheduling conflict with the holidays coming up."

"Oh yes, Jeremy I am fine. Yes, work is going good, de-spite the little bit of drama we had there today." She tried to force him to use some of the manners she worked hard to drill into him, but to no avail. He was on a roll and de-termined to treat her like a pariah. He had changed since the divorce.

True, he was twenty-seven years old, but his parents break up still affected him. She liked to think it wasn't his fault that it turned him into a flaming asshole. Hopefully, he would come to terms with it soon. He showed no prob-lem accepting his new step-mother. She imagined his head flying off and spinning into orbit if he found out about her impromptu engagement to Jericho. She stifled a giggle as he continued as if she never spoken.

"Her parents and my father and Randi will be in attendance." Randi, she knew there was an "I" in her name.

Oh great, she was going to have to deal with the cradle-robber and his new wife. She silently acknowledged what a hypocrite she was as Jericho placed a plate of prawns in front of her.

A very hungry hypocrite.

She mouthed a "Thank you." to Jericho as she listened to her son. "Now I know you are not seeing anyone, and to lessen the awkwardness of having a single person to create an uneven number, I can ask Deacon Philbrick to attend as your escort." she held the phone away from her head to stare at it in disbelief.

What in the hell? No, her son did not just suggest she have a pity date with Deacon Phil*prick* from her old church. He had to be out of his mind if he thought she would voluntarily go anywhere near that handsy ass. She put the phone back up to her ear to hear her son already made arrangements and carried on the conversation as if her agreement was a given.

"Now, just slow your roll there boy." she interrupted him.

"Yes, Mother?" she was about to go through the phone and open up a whole case of whoop-ass on this boy.

"First off, lose the attitude." She saw Jericho stop in the doorway between the dining room and kitchen at these words. He brought out food and placed it on the table as she talked to her son. "I have never now nor never will need you to arrange a date for me." A frown darkened Jericho's face at these words. Ignoring it she carried on with her son. One problem at a time.

"Just text me the information and I will be there and with my fiancé." she got off the phone as fast as possible.

"You're dating someone?" Jericho growled pulling her up out of her seat. Guys and their selective hearing.

"You are mine." He emphasized the statement with a hard kiss to her mouth.

Why was he turning me on? She should be pissed at this man, this young man who was making her lose control of her life. Declaring to her son that she had a fiancé. But instead of getting pissed she was getting wet.

"I am not dating anyone." she replied breathlessly when Jericho ended their kiss only to continue kissing down her throat. "Of course, I'm yours. I just declared you as my fiancé to my son. How much more yours can I get?" His hands had already started working on her blouse to get her breasts free which were heavy with desire. He swept her into his arms, mouth returning to hers as he carried her out of the dining room.

He lifted his head from hers as they moved down a hallway past a large oval window with a fabulous view of Pikes Peak. She looked into his face to see a goofy grin. "Yes, you did. No take backs." He stated before kissing her again.

Chapter Eighteen

JERICHO COULDN'T STOP the need to make Kellista his especially after he overheard her phone conversation with her son. The feeling of possessiveness was bubbling through him.

It was a volcano about to erupt. His cock grew hard as he touched more of her silky satin skin. Hearing her declare him as her fiancé triggered the caveman in him. He swept her up and carried her off to his bedroom.

Dinner was long forgotten.

Kellista was the only thing he wanted to eat. The only thought going through his mind was to get Kellista naked so he could be inside her as soon as possible.

Jericho stopped next to his king size bed. Curiosity covered her face as she looked around his bedroom. He wasn't interested in the décor. He would give her the full tour later if she desired. Right now, he needed to see her naked. He removed her blouse the rest of the way, diverting her attention away from the view of a snow-covered Pikes Peak outside the large picture window making up one wall in Jericho's bedroom. Jericho pushed her skirt down her hips watching in fascination as she shimmied, helping him to remove it. He didn't know what captured his attention more, the movement of her hips or the bouncing of her breasts. The last barrier between him and her skin were gone. His question about her wearing any underwear was answered. That was a firm No. The thought of being in the presence her bare pussy for hours and not being able to touch it struck him. Picking her up, he tossed her on his bed. Slowly he spread her legs wide.

He had to taste her.

He quickly pulled off his clothes. Once he got started nothing was going to stop him. Buttons flew everywhere as he ripped open his shirt. He heard Kellista gasp as his cock sprung free from his pants to stand large and throbbing before her. Once fully exposed, he knelt down on the bed between her thighs. His gaze focused on her pussy and nothing else. His mouth closing over his prize, pulling her legs over his shoulders.

Again, he could feel her high heels digging into his back as she arched up to meet his mouth. He made a mental note to buy her the sexiest heels he could find so she would always have a pair on when he fucked her.

He licked and sucked at his prize. The sounds of Kellista's eager cries spurring him on. He pulled back slightly, to her Kellista cry "no" at the decrease in pressure on her clit.

Jericho grinned against her sweet tasting pussy as he slid a finger into her wet opening. Kellista jerked as he worked his finger in and out of the tight canal and his mouth returned to teasing her clit.

"That's it. Fuck me, yeah fuck me like that!" He heard her scream as he continued to work his finger in and out of her. He added another finger to the mix. This time his finger swept over the secret spot inside of her.

Kellista tightened her legs around his head, grinding her pussy against his mouth and fingers.

A loud shout of "Fuck Yeah!" escaped her as her body tightened around his fingers and convulsed with her orgasm. She stiffened up against him as her orgasm rode her only to end up sagging back on the bed as it finished. The legs trapping Jericho's head loosened. Though he continued to feel the tremors controlling her body.

Jericho's lips made their way across her silken skin. He lightly brushed a kiss across her softly rounded stomach. Easily dodging her hands as she reached for his head, he continued to kiss his way up her body until reaching her mouth.

His mouth dipped to hers. His tongue explored the exotic mixture created by the taste of her pussy and the flavor of her mouth as his hands stroked her body. Her tongue met his stroke for stroke.

He moaned at the taste of her mouth. He cupped her full breasts. Kellista was very responsive to his touch, something he loved about her. She groaned as he pinched her nipple.

He felt her hands smooth across the skin of his back. Gently massaging the area where her heels had dug into him, carried away as she had been with her orgasm. Everywhere she touched was on fire. Just her nails trailing up his spine set his nerve endings on fire. Jericho held her head as he deepened the kiss between them.

He groaned as her hands slide around to his cock.

He couldn't stop the movement of his hips as she stroked him.

Tight squeeze on the upstroke.

Spiral twist on the down stroke.

He didn't think his cock could have gotten any harder, but he was wrong. Her thumb swirled around the tip of his cock spreading the cum leaking from it across the head of his cock. He couldn't wait any longer. He had to be inside of her, NOW.

His cock sought her entrance.

The wetness of her pussy made it easy to slide into her.

Groaning at the tightness surrounding him, he slowly eased into her.

They both groaned as he went balls deep into her.

It was a tighter fit then he remembered.

There was no way he could stay still.

His cock stroked in and out of her hot heat. Building the flames between them hotter.

Higher.

They were in danger of incinerating.

Jericho bent Kellista's knees up changing the angle that his cock was stroking her pussy.

Kellista cried out as he hit her sweet spot.

"Harder!" She demanded.

She moaned when Jericho responded by slamming his cock into her. Each stroke deeper than the one before.

She found herself chanting "Fuck, fuck, fuck!" with each of his strokes.

All she could do was hang on for the ride of her life.

He was waiting for her to reach this point of mindless passion to send her over the edge, Jericho reached down and flicked her clit with his finger. It was still sensitive from the orgasm his mouth caused. It only took one flick to send her over the edge.

Her shout of "Jericho!" was the only warning he received before her pussy clamped down on his cock. Demanding he join her in ecstasy.

He shouted out "Kellista!" as he shot his cum into her pussy. Her pussy continued to milk him long after he thought he was empty.

They collapsed side by side, breathing heavy. A feeling of peace came over him as he gathered Kellista in his arms. He felt true satisfaction came over him as she snuggled closer to him. This was the start of their new life together.

CHAPTER NINETEEN

KELLISTA LAID THERE cuddling in Jericho's arms. She admitted he did look adorable with his head cradled against her breasts as he slept.

How could she explain the feelings he invoked in her? She remembered the initial feeling of lust that came over her when she first set eyes on him, but now she was feeling something intensely more. She truly felt safe. Something she had not experienced since her parents' death. She knew her feelings for Jericho went beyond that of a casual lust. It was deeper than any feeling she ever experienced for Henry. Dare she think of the "L" word? After only one week?

Any of her feelings for Henry died a long time ago. Long before her marriage ended. She could now admit to herself that she stayed married for all those years because it is what was expected of her.

Kellista's parents were old-fashioned and raised their children with their old-fashioned values and morals. The one thing her mother always preached to her was that if there was something wrong in her marriage, then it was because she wasn't being the wife Henry needed. Never once did her mother question if Henry was being the husband Kellista needed. In her mother eyes, it was the wife's duty to keep the marriage together.

It took Kellista a while to really acknowledge that her mother was wrong. It takes two to make a marriage work and no matter how much of an effort she put into the marriage it couldn't be only her. If it was to succeed an equal partnership between both people and both people needed to have their needs met.

Henry's demands for her were to take care of their home and raise their sons with minimal input from him. Not to disrupt his comfort. He was extremely polite to Kellista while showing her hardly any affection. Other than an occasional passionless peck on the cheek. The rare sexual encounter dwindled to nothing after the birth of her last son. Eventually, separate bedrooms had become a norm between them.

It wasn't the shock of discovering Henry having an affair that lead her to finally seek a divorce. No, it was the love and affection he smothered his now new wife in that he denied Kellista all those years as the mother of his sons. Why should she maintain the façade of a happy marriage that obviously stopped being a marriage a long time ago?

Pulling herself from those thoughts, Kellista looked down at Jericho as she stroked her hand through his hair. Then she thought back to what April said.

Was she prepared to let what could possibly be the best thing in my life walk out just because of a number?

Not without giving it her all.

"What are you thinking so hard about?" she had assumed Jericho was sleeping, guess she was wrong.

"You." she teased him.

He slowly opened his eye to look at her. Stupidly sexy blue eye slowly blinked at her.

"What about me?"

"I realize that other than the fact that you know how to send gifts, are awesome in bed, own a club, a kick-ass car, have great taste in chocolate, like to open doors for ladies, and what appears to be a fabulous house, I know nothing about you."

She remembered something else, "I also know you are thirty-two years old. Which makes you five years older than Jeremy, my oldest son."

If she was going to give this relationship a chance then it was time to disregard her earlier misgivings and find out something about her lover. Or was he her fiancé? Especially since she never did deny his claim from earlier today.

"What do you want to know? You can ask me anything. I have nothing to hide from you."

What should she ask first? She pondered as her hand stroked across the answer.

"Who marked you?"

She knew she hit a nerve when Jericho sat up. He climbed out of bed and saunter into the bathroom ignoring her question.

Damn, that man looked good coming and going. There should be a law against an ass that tight, she was momentarily distracted.

He returned a few minutes later wearing a robe.

She whimpered sadly.

He covered up.

He carried another robe in his hands. Reaching to Kellista, he helped her sit up, draping the robe around her.

Kellista was confused as she stood up and tied the robe at her waist. Once that task was completed Jericho clasped her hand in his, their fingers instinctively tangling together as he led her out of the bedroom and towards the kitchen. She really was going to have to look into this habit she was developing of following behind people like a sheep.

CHAPTER TWENTY

JERICHO DIDN'T EXPECT the first question for Kellista to ask would be about his tattoo.

People didn't notice his tatt. He placed behind his ear just for that purpose. To prevent people from asking about it.

Pride coursed through him that she noticed it and she was curious enough to inquire. Most women would have almost immediately asked about his money or his lifestyle if they been given an open-ended option like the one he gave Kellista. Delicious would have been counting the zeros in his bank account if she had been given the same option. Of course someone who sparked such fire in him, would not be so cold.

He led her back into the dining room pulling out her seat for her. The food was exactly where they left it prior to their escapades in the bedroom. He filled a plate for her as he thought about where to start his explanation of the tatt. It was not as simple as telling her the initials.

"Did you cook this?" Kellista looked at the variety of food covering one of the islands behind the fanciest kitchen table she ever seen.

"No," he replied absently, "my chef prepared everything before he left for the night. He didn't know how long we were going to be dealing with the events at your job, so he prepared food that would still taste good and be safe to eat at room temperature. Except the prawns. Those I pulled out the fridge."

"Chef?" he looked at her.

"Yeah, if I have to cook, I would starve to death since cooking was the one thing my mother tried to teach me, but was unable to. Instead she had to declare me hopeless in the kitchen." He said with a grin on his face.

"You're close to your mother?" Here was an opening he could use to explain about the not so simple initials.

"Yeah, for the longest time it was just me and mom." Kellista started eating as he took a deep breath preparing to tell her about the most important person in his life prior to her.

"My mother was an orphan who lost her parents in a car accident when she was a pre-teen." He set his fork down unable to eat while discussing his family.

"She had no living relatives so she went into the system. She moved from foster family to foster family as was the norm with many of the older children in the system. She finally landed with one family that wanted to keep her."

"Little did she know the nicest family she stayed with was the worst family in her life. The family that was supposed to protect her at the very least failed to do so. The foster system that was supposed to care for her failed her too." He looked Kellista directly in the eye to see how she was taking in this information. She too stopped eating. An intense look of concentration on her face as she listened to his story.

Jericho looked back at the food on his plate not really seeing it as he continued on with his story.

"The father. My father had been raping their female foster children. It was discovered by a social worker and investigated, then he went to prison, his wife followed him there. By time it was found out it was too late. My mother was pregnant with me." He couldn't prevent the anger from entering his voice. He looked down in surprise to see Kellista reaching across the table and grabbing his clasped fists gently in her soft hands.

"Unlike some of the other girls under their care, my mother was only in their home for a few months before he was discovered. But that was a few months too long." He took a deep breath before continuing on.

"My mother is amazing." The pride in his voice was unmistakable. "People pressured her to get rid of me. They kept telling her things like 'you don't need a constant reminder of what happened to you around' or 'life with a baby at your age would be too hard', but my mother ignored it all."

"She was sixteen when she gave birth to me. The courts granted her an emancipation. She still managed to take her GED and enrolled in college classes to provide a future for us both."

"She refused to be a victim because of what happened to her and she lavished all of her love on me determined for us to live a good life."

A rueful smile crossed his face. "Her motto was always 'it's you and me against the world, personally I think we are going to get creamed.' she had a nightgown with some cartoon character named Ziggy on it. She wore it proudly, not letting anything stop her." He laughed softly.

"She made a good life for us. We were never rich, but

she managed to go to nursing school and provide for us. She eventually went on to be a sexual assault victim advocate."

He sat there for a minute thinking about his childhood, growing up with just his mom and him. The struggle was real, but he never missed out on anything. He took a deep breath and continued. His hands relaxing from fists twining with Kellista's. He drew support and comfort from her touch.

"The first time I met my father he was serving time in prison down in Canon City. He petitions the court for visitation from me when I was ten years old." It was hard to keep the bitterness from his voice.

"He destroyed my mother's life. He raped her. He impregnated her and left her to raise a child everyone told her to abort. She made a good life for us when the court ordered visitation."

"From the age of ten, I was forced to have court mandated supervised visits. Some asshole of a judge believed I would turn out a better person for knowing my father even if he was in prison for being a serial rapist of underage girls." He heard Kellista's sharply indrawn breath.

"She was devastated. She told me about him being in prison, but she didn't tell me about the rape. That I was the product of rape. To her how I was conceived was not important. Only that I was loved. She worked hard to provide love and a good life for me only for a judge to ruin her hard work by allowing him to force his way into our family." he paused to take a quick drink of the wine. It was too sweet. He needed something stronger. He got up, slipping from her hands and wandered to the cabinet next to the built-in double ovens and pulled out a bottle of A.H. Hirsch Reserve.

He reached up into the cabinet and pulled out two glasses before returning to sit next to Kellista. He poured a dollop in each glass.

"For six years I was forced to visit this asshole only to listen to him justify his actions by saying the girls enticed him." he couldn't keep the disgust out of his voice. He tossed back his glass of bourbon. He smiled as he watched Kellista first sniff what was in the glass and then take a tentative sip of it. He rubbed her back as she started coughing.

Kellista took a deep breath and then tossed back the bourbon as Jericho did immediately falling into a coughing fit. Jericho continued to rub her back. She reached up to wipe the tears from her watering eyes. "Smooth." She managed to cough out.

"On my last visit, I was sixteen years old. I had had enough. I wasn't going to listen to his lies anymore. I told him he was a dirty bastard who deserved to die in prison. The next time I would see him was to spit on his grave." He smiled softly, just a little pain tinging it.

"Then I went out and got this tattoo in honor of my mother and her strength."

Kellista moved from her seat to sit on his lap. It felt right to have her on his lap. He put his arms around her engulfing her.

She was the first woman he ever told, or even opened up to about his past. The first and only. Overwhelming rightness filled him.

Kellista's touch soothed him. Having her fingers running through his hair helped him to release the anger he kept bottled up in him. An anger he would never burden his mother with. Anger he truly had not known weighed on him until it was freed.

"Where is your mother now?" Kellista asked him. He chuckled.

"She met a great guy named Gary, married him and moved to Florida. They own a surf shop on the beach. I am also the proud owner of two high school age younger brothers." Jericho laughed once more at thoughts of some of his younger brothers' antics.

"Gary is the only father I ever really had. He taught me how to be a man and how to treat a woman right."

He lifted her chin so he could look into her eyes, "You asked who taught me how to do gift giving? I learned from the example Gary provided me when I was growing up."

He continued to lock eyes with Kellista. "When are going to marry me?" Yes, he popped the question while they sat in their robes eating dinner just a week after meeting. Hell, he already exposed his soul to her. He had no more secrets. He felt in his gut, and he just knew she was the one for him. Now he just needed to convince her he was the one for her.

CHAPTER TWENTY-ONE

KELLISTA CAN HONESTLY say the second marriage proposal she received in her life was a lot different than the first. Granted she was wearing a robe while sitting on Jericho's lap as he finished explaining one of the saddest things to happen, when he popped the question. But it was an improvement over the last proposal she received.

To this day she would swear Henry grunted the word, "Marriage" and she just agreed because it was expected of her.

She just couldn't quite get her mouth to speak.

Being stunned was the least of the feelings coursing through her.

"You know what?" she looked warily at Jericho waiting to see what would come out of his mouth next, "Put the thought on hold for now. We will revisit this conversation in the future. We will just enjoy our engagement for now."

Kellista wasn't used to someone taking charge. Usually she was the one who made all of the decisions. She was fascinated listening to Jericho plan their lives together. He was so confident she would agree to not only the engagement, but also eventually a marriage.

He nodded, then Jericho changed the subject and told her about growing up with Gary. Even though the topic changed, she couldn't stop the thought of marriage to Jericho from floating around her head.

What would marriage be like with a strong partner?

Her heart and mind were at war. Her mind telling her to say no, but her heart was telling her say yes.

"Stop thinking about it." Jericho ordered. As if it was that simple. Kellista made a conscious effort to put it from her mind, but in a small part of it, way in the back a little voice yelled "yes".

Kellista continued sitting on Jericho's lap feeding him food as they talked well into the night. It was a good everything happened on a Friday, otherwise there was no way she was going to make it to work in the morning.

She told him about her marriage and about her three sons. She told him about Janet, her son Jeremy's fiancé and how much she liked her. Especially the fact she didn't take any of Jeremy's pretentious shit.

"Besides your marriage. Is there any other thing you regret not having done in life?" Jericho knew how to ask the tough questions.

She released a sigh as she thought over the things that had occurred in her life. Surprisingly, her marriage going south wasn't the thing she regretted.

"I regret never having a daughter." She stared into the fireplace. They moved from the kitchen area to the living room and Jericho turned on the fireplace. There was something intimate about telling all of your secrets in the glow of a fire. It created a cocoon. Their own intimate world where anything was possible.

"I love my sons, but there is a special bond between a daughter and her mother. Even though my mother was bat-shit crazy, we had a relationship that was different from my father. I regret not experiencing the same thing with my own daughter." she gave a soft laugh.

"But given how my boys turned out maybe it is a good thing I didn't have a daughter."

"You can't be blamed for your sons." Jericho said to her, "Their father also played a role in raising them so the good and the bad has to be shared between the two of you. It is not fair just he receives all the credit for the good and you get all the credit for the bad."

She leaned her head against Jericho's, "You are very wise."

"When life throws shit at you you learn to look at both sides of the equation." He kissed her forehead.

She continued to cuddle next to him on the sofa absorbing the wisdom he imparted. She need to do something to lighten the mood, she couldn't help thinking.

They had both shared intimate knowledge of our past.

It was more potent than the sharing of their bodies and they needed time to think. To come to terms with what they discussed.

Kellista lifted her head from his shoulder where it came to rest while they held their discussion,

"You wanna tell me how is it you own this gorgeous house." she seriously wanted to know.

A sheepish look came over Jericho's face as he looked around the living room. "When I bought the house, I bought it with the thought of having a family. I know it is a little big for one person."

"Yeah, but seriously are you selling drugs out of your clubs or something to afford this?"

Kellista knew she had made a mistake as soon as the words left her lips. She needed to kick her own ass.

The affronted look on Jericho's face confirmed it. "I do not do, let alone sell drugs." The icy tone of his voice was enough to freeze Kellista to her bones. She fucked up. Perhaps it was the fears of their relationship that inspired such a rude question. Her curiosity about him came out harsher than she had intended. She had been trying to lighten the mood between while getting some much-desired answers.

"I am sorry I said that." A look of sorrow crossed her face.

The happy playful look that resided on Jericho's face was replaced by a stone face that genuinely intimidated her. She may have been older than Jericho, but the harsh lessons that life dealt him far surpassed anything she ever experienced. She really had led a sheltered life.

Though the look on Jericho's face intimidated her she knew in her heart he would never hurt her. It was obvious as he continued to rub soothing circles on her back. Another habit of his that she enjoyed.

She reached out and stroked his hair. She knew this motion soothed him before, she hoped it would work this time. A shudder went through him, the tension eased from him and he relaxed back down on the sofa. Cuddling Kellista once again.

"I got my bachelors in business and an MBA from UCLA." He started to relax even more, he was not back to the level he been at before her insult but he was slowly returning.

"While I was in Cali I would club hop with the best of them. I started to notice which clubs were popular and packed night after night. I decided if I was going to run a business I would run a profitable and entertaining one while I was at it."

Jericho paused long enough to place a soft kiss on her lips.

"I gathered backing from friends and opened my first night club in downtown LA. With the club's success, I was able to pay my backers. I sold it for a tidy profit. Half of the money I invested and the other half I opened my next club. When that became profitable I sold it and moved back to Colorado Springs."

"When I opened Club Envy I decided not to just cater to the night life of the Springs, but also the elite jet setting crowd that came to Colorado for the outdoor activities. At the same time my investments were also paying off. The tech companies I invested in took off, a clothing line I backed became big in menswear."

"Is that the *Johan* that Office Wilder was going crazy about?" She interrupted.

"Yeah, *Johan* or Lathan as I call him. We met when I was at UCLA. He was working for some designer in Cali. We met at a party where he nearly had a heart attack at my atrocious clothing." Jericho made air quotes as he remembered his friend reaction. "He insisted he dress me the next day. From there we became roommates and friends. When I relocated to Colorado he came also. He didn't have any true ties in Cali." He chuckled.

"He continues to dress me to this day even though his clothing line is a major success and he has long paid off his loan. I have to send a check to his assistant to pay for my clothes because he still insists on giving me my clothes even though I have enough money to afford his clothing."

"Exactly what kind of numbers are we talking?" the curiosity at his success couldn't be contain. She had no idea it was possible to build wealth with technology though she would admit it was probably her own fault. Technology scared her and she tended to shy away from things that scared her. Case in point. Her committing fully to Jericho. Who in their right mind jumped into a relationship with someone they only knew for a week and a day, officially.

"Oh, it's not much just a few." he avoided looking her directly in the eyes.

She knew he was not telling her everything. Jericho was a very direct person. His habit of looking a person directly in the eye was one of the things she admired about him.

"Jericho...." she dragged out the sound of his name.

"What?" he tried to look innocent, but all he did was make him look adorable.

"A few what?"

"Just a few billion." he mumbled.

"Billion?" she shrieked.

He gave a resigned sigh and gave her his direct look.

"Yes, billions. One of the clean energy companies I invested in went big years ago making me a huge profit."

Kellista couldn't help it she was stunned. She was having sex with a thirty-two-year-old billionaire. It was great, hot, pussy dampening sex, but it was with a billionaire.

Jericho grabbed a hold of her chin and kissed her hard on the mouth. She moaned into his mouth at the taste of him. Relaxing into the kiss, twining her hands in his hair.

"I didn't tell you because I didn't want to give you another excuse to run from me." he murmured against her throat as he trailed kisses down her neck.

"Yeah, that was probably a smart move." she groaned. Jericho pulled back away looking at her in surprise.

"What? That was a smart move and you were probably right in thinking I would have ran for the hills if you had told me this when we first met."

Jericho groaned as he swept her up into his arms carrying her back to his bedroom. Once there he showed her how smart he was and especially how clever he could be with his tongue and fingers.

CHAPTER TWENTY-TWO

AFTER THAT SOUL sharing night, Jericho and Kellista shifted into a comfortable routine, spending a majority of their time together. She started frequenting Club Envy to spend time with him while he worked. His staff loved her. Malcolm even deigned to inform him that "Miss Kellista was a very good addition to his life." That was the most personal statement that he ever received from Malcom. He was truly impressed. The only time they didn't spend together was when she worked at her job. He couldn't exactly hang around the human resource department of her company. Then she would never get any work done.

No more mysterious packages were delivered to her job. Though after weeks of investigating the police still didn't have any leads on who sent it. There were no markings on the box to indicate where it came from.

Jericho lost the argument time and again about Kellista moving in with him. She maintained she lived by herself for less than a year and she was going to enjoy her little house. The argument didn't make sense to Jericho since they were practically attached at the hips, but after one too many rounds, he stopped arguing with her about it. At least for the time being.

As the holidays approached, nothing changed, they even spent the Thanksgiving holiday together. It was a big step in their relationship when he took her to Florida to meet his family. He worked hard to convince her to go and Kellista nervousness was obvious the whole flight. He took advantage of her lack of experience with first class, distracting her from her nerves.

Kellista enjoyed all of the perks the flight attendant offered during the three-hour flight to Atlanta. The first-class lounge at the Atlanta airport was a novelty for her, as was the last leg of the flight. Jericho was sure she would have relaxed more if she drank something, but she was afraid of meeting his family intoxicated so she stuck to bottled water.

For the first few moments of the meeting at the airport she'd been on edge. Jericho thought for sure he was going to lose a hand, she squeezed it so tightly. The awkwardness lasted as long as it took for her to meet his mother, Sharon and his step-father Gary.

Kellista held out her hand to shake his mother's when Sharon grabbed Kellista in a big hug. She was such a tiny thing that Kellista felt like she was towering over her. She could then see where Jericho got his stunning blue eyes from. Her short sassy haircut reminded Kellista of the elves she would read about in the books she had as a child. Yes, meeting Sharon, she could understand Jericho's desire to protect a woman. Her fragile appearance was deceptive. Kellista knew that she had a core of steel to survive all that life had thrown at her and to continue living instead of being buried under the weight of it all.

"Oh, Kellista I am so happy to meet you!" Sharon, Jericho's mother, squeezed Kellista, a huge grin on her face. "I was so excited when Jericho said you were coming with him for the holiday. I have heard so much about you."

"You have?" Kellista wasn't sure if this was a good thing or a bad thing.

She released Kellista only for Kellista to find herself scooped up into Gary's arms for another hug. "We are so glad you both are here."

"Oh yes. I was just so happy that he was not bringing home that Delicious girl. She is such a THOT." Sharon said as they gathered their luggage.

"A THOT?" Kellista cut a sideways glance at Jericho wondering if he knew what his mother had just said.

Jericho just grinned at her and shrugged. "Oh yes, my younger sons taught me that term. They said it described her accurately." She gave a decisive nod. Sharon continued to chat during the short ride from the airport to their beach front home. That started the friendly tone of the visit off right.

The holiday flew by with Kellista falling more and more in love with Jericho's family. They welcomed her with open arms. She enjoyed the novelty of having a holiday without snow and with Palm Trees.

Thanksgiving Day, Kellista and Sharon spent in the kitchen cooking. From the amount of laughter that was coming from the area, Jericho knew that they were fast becoming best friends. Jericho had even heard his mother refer to Kellista as her "little sister". She was holding it over Kellista that she was eleven months older than her. Kellista had jokingly replied, "Great, just what I need. One more older sister. The two I have aren't enough?" Rolling her eyes at the ceiling.

Thanksgiving dinner laughter filled as they all sat around the table eating. Gary had brought tears to Kellista's eyes when he had given thanks for bringing her to Jericho and making her a welcome addition to their family. She had not expected such unconditional acceptance from his family. The acceptance went both ways. She teased Jericho's younger brothers, Troy and Todd, as if she had known them all of their lives.

The night before they were due to fly out to return to Colorado, Sharon and Gary sat with them on the back porch watching the sunset over the ocean as Troy and Todd decorated the palm trees with Christmas lights.

"Kellista, I have watched you and Jericho together for the past few days." Sharon spoke into the quiet evening. "At first when he told me that he was dating an older woman I was concerned." She paused long enough to reach out and take Kellista's hand into hers. "I thought you would be just like the rest of the gold-digging woman who only want Jericho for what he could give them and not for himself."

She looked into Kellista's eyes a tear sparkling in the corner, but not falling. "I was so happy to see that you love my son. That is all I ever wanted for him was for someone to love him as he deserves. And I am happy that he found that love in you. I am glad that the two of you have found each other and even though you don't need it I do give your relationship my blessing."

Kellista sat stunned at her statement. She hugged Sharon. She had not known how much Sharon acceptance of her meant to her. But knowing that she was unconditionally accepted into Jericho's family was an unexpected gift, something for her to cherish.

She was quiet on the return trip to Colorado. Absorbing what his mother had said to her. When they were dropped off at his house by the car service she gave him a huge hug and a small smile. It was a turning point in their relationship. After that, a more relaxed Kellista emerged. To Jericho it was another obstacle out of his way of convincing Kellista to have something more permanent. Their engagement was becoming something more than a hastily said statement during a police interrogation.

Thinking over all the changes that had happened, Jericho made a mental note to get into contact with Jessica Wield, Kellista's attorney, to see how things were progressing with Kellista's case. Delicious was still making a nuisance of herself, by giving interviews to anyone with a blog about her "engagement" to Jericho. According to his publicist as soon as her team squashed one of Delicious's rumors another one popped up. She mentioned taking legal actions against her, but Jessica recommended they wait until after Kellista's case was handled.

Jericho only agreed to wait because Kellista agreed to wait. Though he did contact his friends and let them know all of the statements that Delicious was making were false. They offered him support as he knew they would.

"Ryder." answering his office phone as he continued to go over some new marketing information.

"Blue." Kellista's husky voice came through the phone.

"Hello, darling." He knew Kellista was in a playful mood by the sound of her voice. They had been getting to know each other very well during the past few weeks. Learning each other's likes and dislikes.

Moods.

After that one tense night, of passion and sharing, there had been no more mention of their age difference. No mention of his wealth, though she insisted that she pay for some of their activities. He thought it was cute.

She insisted this was an equal partnership and that she was going to contribute also or they were just wasting their time.

She surprised him. She was the only woman he dated who didn't automatically let him pay for everything once she found out how much money he made.

She also didn't expect gifts.

She continued to bitch at him about the amount he spent on the gifts he continued to send to her office.

He smiled as he remembered her reaction to the Black Amex card he given her with her name on it. His ears still burned from the bitching out she gave him. He reached up to touch the healing cut in his forehead from the card hitting him when she threw it at him.

That memory led to another, how she made up for cutting him after she bandaged him up made his cock stiffen. It was probably guilt from his injury keeping her from mentioning the card again after he secretly slipped it into her wallet.

"Blue what, darling?"

"Underwear."

"What?" he said sitting up quickly, now 100% focused on her statement.

"I am wearing blue underwear today."

"You evil, evil, wench." He heard her laughing as she hung up the phone on him. Well he would beat her at her own game.

CHAPTER TWENTY-THREE

KELLISTA WAS IN yet another meeting with Crystal and a recovered Rob when her office door flew open. Her mouth dropped in shock at seeing Jericho standing there. Only thirty minutes had passed since her naughty phone call to him.

He looked at her assistants with a feral look on his face. "Get out."

She sat there in shock watching them gather up their stuff and scuttle out of the office. Jericho slamming the door behind them locking it.

The feral look on his face changed to one of hunger as he stalked across her office. Being his pray had yet to have a downside.

She stood up to confront him.

"Now Jericho…" she started only to be shushed by him.

She tried to ignore her pussy's response to such an autocratic gesture. She reached deep inside her for some righteous anger, but could only find a burning desire accompanied by a gush of wetness soaking the blue panties she had teased him about.

She was not going to facing him sitting down. She learned that lesson and was not going to be at such a disadvantage again.

"What the hell…." Was as far as she got before Jericho was on her. Pulling her into his arms, his mouth on hers as a deep, soul stealing kiss ensued.

She was dazed.

She was on fire, a fire only Jericho could put out.

Jericho spun her around, pressing her over her desk. It was not a solid oak desk like the one in his office, but a cool metal desk prevalent in many office buildings.

Cool air hit her ass, a counterpoint to his warm hands sliding across her skin as he pushed her skirt up to rip off the inciting pair of blue panties. The sound of his zipper loud to her ears, causing an increase in wetness.

Jericho's cock slammed into her. Kellista cried out at the friction caused by his cock rubbing her pussy walls. Her body craved his touch. The tension growing with each of his hard strokes.

"Fuck me!"

"Fuck my pussy hard!" Jericho did as Kellista demanded and fucked her harder. Hard enough to scoot her desk with each of his cock pounding thrusts. Kellista thought it was thrilling to be fucked on Jericho's desk, but there was something even more exhilarating about being fucked on her own desk. Her co-workers being just a few steps away.

She screamed "Jericho!" as she came, sagging against her desk.

Her pussy squeezing his cock strongly enough to pull an answering groan from him.

Jericho wasn't through with her though.

Jericho sat down heavily in her office chair. His cock still buried deep in her pussy as she spasmed around him. Her skirt was up around her waist, the scraps of her panties, dangling around her ankles.

The buttons of her blouse were coming open from his rough treatment. Jericho's hand pinched and pulled her nipple into a hard nub.

Her boss could have walked into her office and seen her wanton display and she wouldn't have cared. All she cared about was the cock buried deep in her pussy and the ache that could only be satisfied by him.

She moaned as she rode Jericho's thick hard cock.

Tits bouncing with every thrust.

Cries escaped her lips with each thrusting of his cock.

"Yes, baby. Ride my hard cock."

"Who's fucking your brains out?" he gritted out from between his clenched teeth, thrusting deep into her.

"You are." she said breathlessly.

"Who?" he demanded pulling her head back and capturing her mouth. He tilted Kellista's ass up higher so he could go deeper. Kellista let out a loud shout at the new angle. That was unexpected, he now knew he hit her sweet spot. Nothing could stop him from hitting it over and over again. Each time he passed over it Kellista's pussy tightened on his cock.

"Who?" he demanded again when his mouth released hers from the passion inflaming kiss.

"Jericho!" She screamed as she orgasmed. Her pussy squeezing his cock. Cum shot into her pussy forcibly. She felt it all throughout her spasming pussy, bathing her insides and prolonging her orgasm.

Jericho shout her name as he shot load after load of cum into her.

Shudders rolled through her as her pussy squeezed and fluttered around his cock.

She collapsed back onto Jericho trying to catch her breath. Jericho's petted her, soothing her down from her shattering orgasm.

She was more than a little surprised when Jericho started gently cleaning her up with his handkerchief. What guy carried a handkerchief in this day and age?

He straightened her skirt, buttoning her blouse back up before gently placing her back in her chair. Smirking he pushed it up close to her desk.

She watched as he fixed his clothing and then straightened her desk without saying anything.

He placed a soft kiss on her mouth before walking to her door, pausing only to unlock it. He turned back to her a smirk on his face.

"I love the blue underwear." He sauntered out her office stuffing what was left of her underwear in his pocket.

She stared at the door in a "fucked" daze.

Chapter Twenty-Four

KELLISTA CHEWED HER bottom lip absently as she left work. After the incident in her office, she had been too embarrassed to continue the meeting. Now though, as she walked out she looked to the spot where Jericho usually parked his Mercedes SUV.

She didn't see it.

Jericho had developed the habit of picking her up from work when her car been in the shop and continued it even after it was returned to her. Maybe he had driven something other than the SUV. After all, he had several other vehicles he could be driving. He mentioned the Mercedes was his goto winter vehicle because it handled well in bad weather.

She dodged a pile of snow left from the sidewalk cleaning thanks to the snowstorm earlier in the week.

She looked around the area and didn't see his Mercedes SUV. The red vehicle was hard to miss in the winter twilight. One time, she made the mistake of calling it a car and received a long lecture on how it was not just a car, but a superior machine.

This memory brought a faint smile, but was not enough to pull her mind away from the disturbing conversation she just finished with one of the vice-presidents of the company. He had called her into his office to discuss a complaint of prejudice that came against her through their employee whistleblowing line.

Though the man stated they did not believe the allegations they were still required to investigate it by company policy. Company policy also stated she had to be suspended following these allegations while an investigation was conducted. Either the allegations would be proven false and she could return to work, or they gathered sufficient information to terminate her employment. He waited until as late today as possible to inform her of this development. This way he could start her suspension at the time she started her Christmas vacation.

He had seemed genuinely sorry about delivering such news right before the Christmas, but he was sure they would have the situation cleared up by time she returned from her vacation.

Of course, he couldn't give her any information about who made the accusations. It was company policy to keep the person reporting misconduct's identity confidential to prevent any sort of retaliation. Though, he could tell her it was reported that she had made several derogatory remarks against her white colleagues during new employee orientation.

Kellista had been shocked to hear about the accusations. She had never made any type of racist comments towards anyone in her life. She grown up hearing about her parent's struggle living in a small racist town in the deep south. People treated them as less because of their skin color. She vowed to never judge anyone because of something they could not control.

Her thoughts swirled around her head causing her to lose focus on her surroundings. Reality rushed back at the sound of feet rushing towards her. Standing in front of her office building in downtown Colorado Springs waiting for Jericho not really paying attention was not her brightest idea.

Many people left early to start their Christmas celebrations, leaving the usually bustling area deserted. As she turned towards the sound, wondering if someone needed help, she was grabbed from behind, her mouth covered as she was dragged into the alley between the office building and the parking garage next to it. It was too early for the downtown club crowd, and with her building deserted there was no one to witness what was happening.

She didn't fight her attacker.

"Give me your purse, Bitch!" he demanded.

Kellista handed it over willingly. There was nothing in the cheap handbag she couldn't be replaced. The only thing of real value in her purse was Jericho's black AMEX card. It would easily be canceled before her attacker could charge anything.

Jericho would simply see her loss of her handbag as an excuse to take her shopping and buy her something expensive that would make her eyes bulge out of her head at the price.

The guy pushed Kellista against the brick wall. Kellista slipped on the ice that formed when the temperature dropped. Her attacker grabbed her by the hair smacking her face first into the wall leaving her dazed. The left side of her face was in pain from the force of hitting the brick wall. She could already feel the swelling develop. He pulled her up by the hair and spinning her around causing more dizziness at the sudden movement.

"Now to do what I was paid for." a menacing voice emerged from her attacker's throat. Kellista heard the click of a switchblade opening. She could see her impending death in his eyes. This was not a simple mugging this was something more. Her mind flashed to thoughts of Jericho. How she would miss out on having him in her life. How her death would affect him.

She thought of all the time she wasted being scared.

Scared of what people would think.

Scared of the future.

Scared of risking her heart again.

She was not ready to give up.

'Who the hell carries a switchblade now days?' She thought. *'This is Colorado everyone owns a gun.'*

The feel of the cold metal against her throat cleared her mind a little.

No.

She was not ready to give up.

She reached up and grabbed the outside of his right wrist, the one holding the knife, with her right hand as her attacker tried to apply pressure to slice her throat. Using her Capoeira training Kellista reached under his wrist with her left hand grabbing his right wrist. She twisted her attacker's wrist under and back away from her throat, forcing him to release the knife.

Angered at the unexpected resistance from his victim the attacker reached his free left hand up and slammed her head against the side of the building with tremendous force causing Kellista to slump to the ground.

'Jericho' her mind whispered before it shut down.

CHAPTER TWENTY-FIVE

JERICHO'S SUV SLOWED down as he approached her building, just beyond the open alleyway. He was late due to an accident on interstate 25 forcing him to detour. He called Kellista earlier to give her a heads up, but she hadn't answered her phone. He hoped she listened to his message to stay in the building since it was now dark. He felt more comfortable if he came inside to get her.

He was almost to her building when he glanced down the alleyway to see a large figure attacking a smaller one. He slammed on the breaks and jumped out of his vehicle running across the icy road to help the victim.

The attacker was too busy delivering a brutal kick to the victim down on the ground that he didn't hear Jericho's approach until Jericho slammed into him causing him to lose his balance on the ice and slam into the wall.

"What the fuck?" the attacker yelled turning on Jericho.

Jericho delivered a punch to the attacker face. A feeling of satisfaction overcoming him at the audible crack to the attacker's nose and the gush of blood.

"No amount of money is worth this." The attacker yelled grabbing Kellista's purse off the ground and rushing off. He jumped in Jericho's still running Mercedes, squealing the tires as he drove off.

Jericho was not worried about his car, instead turning his attention to the victim. His eyes took in the familiar looking coat.

"Kellista!" he yelled realizing it was his woman under attack from the unknown thug.

He reached down to carefully lift her face towards him, patting her gently on the cheek. He touched her body trying to locate where she was injured. It wasn't until he reached up to move her head away from the wall he noticed the blood staining it. It hadn't been visible in the dark shadows of the alley. The street lights were now casting a large enough glow.

He reached into his pocket and pulled out his cellphone.

"Hold on baby, I will get you some help." He pushed the app on his phone waiting impatiently for someone to answer.

"How may I assist you, Mr. Ryder?" The voice on the other end of the app answered his emergency call.

"I have a woman with me who appears to be suffering from a head injury." He said, louder than intended as he looked at her on the ground.

"Was this a vehicle accident?" the voice asked calmly.

"No, it was a mugging and the mugger stole my vehicle." He wanted to pick Kellista up off of the cold ground, but he knew if the mugger injured her neck then he would cause more damage by moving her then leaving her on the cold, hard ground.

"Hold on, darling." He muttered softly to her, "I got

you. Nothing will happen to you again."

"An ambulance is being dispatched to your location Mr. Ryder." The voice spoke again. "We see your Mercedes SUV coupe is in motion. With your permission, we will notify the police so they can apprehend the person who took your vehicle."

"Yeah, go ahead and do what you have to do. Just get the ambulance here quickly." Even as he finished speaking he could hear the sound of sirens. He looked up to see flashing lights of a firetruck in the entrance of the alleyway. Firefighters piled out of the vehicle to assist her.

He stepped out of the way as they started attending Kellista and asking him questions.

He heard a soft groan as Kellista started to regain consciousness. The firefighters tried to question her but she mumbled something and lost consciousness again. Jericho explained about the attack as they loaded her on the gurney from the ambulance which had finally arrived on the scene.

Nobody even tried to stop him as he climbed in the back of the ambulance with Kellista. He clasped her hand as a paramedic worked on her. He watched silently as they hooked her up to monitors and spoke with dispatch as they hurried to the trauma center.

CHAPTER TWENTY-SIX

JERICHO LET GO of Kellista's hand when they arrived at the trauma center. He continued into the trauma center following behind her gurney until a nurse stopped him as they wheeled her into an exam room.

"Only family can accompany her beyond this point." the nurse stated.

Jericho dead-eyed her. "I am her fiancé." He stated. He saw the nurse look him up and down and then looked over at Kellista. A look of judgement crossed her face closely followed by distaste as she took in obvious difference of their skin. Before she could say anything, another nurse stuck his head out from behind the swinging doors leading into the triage area looking around. He gestured towards Jericho when his gaze alighted on him.

"Mr. Ryder the Doctor has requested your presence." He swung the door open wide clearly expecting him to accompany him.

Jericho gave the other nurse a cold look before proceeding. He stopped turning around. "What is your name?" he inquired in a voice cold enough to rival the temperature outside.

"My name is Phyllis Duncan." she replied.

"Well Ms. Duncan. I hope you enjoy your shift, because if I have anything to do it with this will be the last one you work here. That means if I have to donate a new wing to get your ass fired, then a new wing it will be." He turned on his heel following the wide-eyed male nurse.

Jericho didn't like to throw his money around, especially using it to ruin other people's life; but the last thing grieving relatives needed to deal with was her judgmental ass making life difficult. He would have to find out what kind of nurse she was. Maybe she could do with a refresher in cultural sensitivity. It would come in handy for the diverse cultures that made up Colorado Springs.

"Does she have any allergies?" the question was fired at him the moment he entered the area Kellista was in. He saw she had been changed into a hospital gown and was hooked up to even more equipment then she had been in the ambulance. The sight of all of the wires and tubes coming from her was enough to make Jericho's heart stop.

"No, she doesn't have any allergies." he replied trying to stay calm to help. Some of the tension left him when he saw one of the people working her was his close friend Doctor Sebastian Croft. Also known as Doctor Sebastian by the staff and patients of the trauma center.

"The paramedics said she regained consciousness in the ambulance a couple of times. Do you know how hard her head was hit?"

"I don't know. She was already unconscious when I found her."

"What was she doing when she lost consciousness?" one of the other doctor working over her asked.

"I am going to take a wild guess and say she was being attacked." Jericho didn't stop the sarcasm from entering his voice when he responded.

"Jericho." Sebastian warned him. He looked up from Kellista and took his arm leading him out of the room. "We need to do a CT scan on her to see if she has a skull fracture or any bleeding on the brain."

"Well do it." Jericho demanded. "Do whatever you need to in order for Kellista to wake up. I can't live without her, Sebastian." He grabbed ahold of Sebastian's lab coat.

Sebastian grabbed ahold of Jericho's hand prying them from his coat. "It's not that simple."

"Why not?" he demanded.

"Kellista is pregnant." Sebastian grabbed Jericho as all of the color drained from his face.

"What? Why didn't she tell me?" he was shocked. His heart breaking at the possibility of Kellista keeping such news from him.

"She may not even be aware of it." Sebastian told him. "We know because it is routine to run a test on unconscious females of childbearing age prior to them having a CT scan."

"Jericho, it is possible the dye from the CT scan can cause harm to the fetus. We need your permission to continue. Assuming you are the father?" Sebastian continued.

"Yes." he whispered as the thought of being a father sunk in. "Yes, she is pregnant with my child!"

"What happens if you don't run the CT?" he had to know his options.

"If she has a skull fracture or bleeding then we won't know until it is too late to treat it. Meaning, Kellista could die." Sebastian was blunt when he delivered the news. Jericho knew the lack of emotion in his voice bellied the seriousness of Kellista's condition.

This was one of the most difficult decisions Jericho had to make. Either he authorized the CT scan and possibly killed his own child or he didn't and possibly lose the love of his life.

'And his child', his mind tacked on.

His heart seized at the thought of losing Kellista. She had become such a big part of his life that the thought of living without her was enough to stop his heart.

"Do the CT." he finally told Sebastian. There was a risk to the baby if they did the CT, but there was a bigger risk to the baby if Kellista died because they didn't do the CT.

He didn't want to lose his child, but he only knew about the baby for five minutes. Without the CT, he was almost guaranteed to lose them both.

"Doctor Sebastian, the patient is awake." the male nurse called out from Kellista's room. Jericho rushed back into the room to see Kellista laying on the gurney, her right eye open. The left one swollen shut. Injured in the attack, most likely.

He perked up when he heard a faint groan. "Jericho?"

Even though Kellista's voice could barely be heard it was enough to make his knees weak.

"I am here, darling." he clasped her free hand. The nurse put an IV in her other one. "You're going to be alright."

"Where am I?"

"You're at the hospital."

"Why?"

"You were attacked and Sebastian is treating you." Jericho told her.

"Hey, Sebastian." Kellista said faintly recognizing Jericho's doctor friend.

"Hey Kellista." Sebastian said quietly back, but Kellista's

eyes already closed as she drifted off to sleep.

Jericho looked at one of his closest friends with tears in his eyes. Silently he was begging him to fix his heart.

"Let's get her to CT." Sebastian acknowledge the silent plea.

CHAPTER TWENTY-SEVEN

JERICHO PACED THE hallway while Kellista was in the CT scan. After the CT scan, they moved Kellista from the trauma center to a private room at his insistence. Her insurance would only cover the cost of a semi-private room, but he demanded a room just for her. Stating to the admitting staff, he personally would cover any of the cost for her care that her insurance did not cover including the cost of a private room. What was the point of having billions if he could not use them to make Kellista as comfortable as possible?

He entered the hospital room, having stepped out to contact Kellista's older sister Cynthia to update her on Kellista. Seeing Kellista laying there on the bed looking like a fragile doll pained him.

His heart broke.

Emotions were overwhelming him. He thought back to the moment he found her laying there, slumped in the alley. The bastard mugger drawing back his foot to kick her. All of the worry and pain at the thought of him losing her came rushing back at the memory. He clasped her free hand in his and brought it to his lips.

"Even though you can't hear me, I have to tell you my heart stopped when I thought I might lose you. You're the best thing to come into my life and I am going to spend every day from now on convincing you to spend forever with me." He reached up wiping a tear from his eye. "I love you Kellista." He bent down kissing her cheek softly as she slept on the hospital bed.

He settled back into the seat next to her bed holding her hand, waiting for her to wake up again and to tell him she was going to be all right. There wasn't a chance of him moving, he was here for the long haul.

Hours later, Kellista finally opened her eyes to see she was in a different hospital room than the one she been in before. She saw Jericho sitting in a chair next to her bed staring intently at his cellphone. She would have felt neglected if she hadn't felt the firm grasp of his hand in her hand.

She thought back on the words she had heard him speak when she drifted off to sleep earlier.

Jericho loves me.

She felt the warmth inside her heart, Jericho had snuck his way into her heart becoming more and more important to her, as important to her as her sons. He was a big part of her now. It surprised her at how fast and suddenly it had happened.

This new awareness made her realize she'd finally been truthful with herself. It wasn't Jericho's age keeping her from fully committing to a relationship with him.

No, it was fear.

Fear of giving her heart away. Fear it would open it up to being stomped on. She finally realized even though Henry had bruised it and kicked it around it still had the capacity to truly love.

What she felt for Jericho went much deeper than anything she ever felt for Henry. He had the power to destroy her like nothing else in this world ever did. She let out a deep breath and with it let go of the fear holding her back from Jericho.

She was no longer going to let fear rule her. She was going to grab ahold of Jericho and hold on tight to him. She was going to live a life full of love and in order to do so she needed Jericho.

The small sound was enough to draw Jericho's attention.

Immediately he set his phone down, bringing her hand up to his mouth while turning it over to place a kiss in the palm. The same motion he had done the first time they met. He stood up next to her bed.

"How are you feeling?" he asked her softly.

She groaned as she shifted on the bed, "Like someone ran over me, backed up over me, and then ran over me again."

"Well you did kind of look like you were under the weather when I first saw you today."

"How long have I been out?" Kellista asked.

"A few hours." she was surprised by Jericho's answer. She looked towards the window seeing stars. It must be the middle of the night.

"Have you been with me all this time?" her heart swelled with love at his silent nod.

"I love you." she softly whispered to him.

She felt his grip tighten at those words. Jericho bent his head down until their foreheads were touching. A tear dropped from his face onto hers. She reached up and pulled him close to her. Basking in the love he was conveying to her with his touch. Their hearts binding to each other as she let down the final wall standing between them.

"I love you so much." he whispered to her the emotion present and clear in his voice. "I thought I was going to lose you." Jericho finally felt like it was time to truly confess the depth of his feelings for her. The fear of losing her had been real, the chance there, and it had terrified him. It was something his heart demanded he do.

"I will love you for this life, and into the next." His heart swelled at the wealth of emotions in Kellista's words. Everything he fought for, every battle, the worry all culminated into this moment. She was worth the wait and the struggle. He pressed his mouth against Kellista's for a sweet, gentle kiss.

He didn't know how long they stayed like that. It could have been a few minutes or it could have been forever. They were interrupted by a soft knock on the door and the entrance of Sebastian and another doctor.

"I see our patient is awake." Sebastian said as he came to stand next to Jericho at Kellista's bedside. "How are you feeling?"

"Other than a major headache and my face hurts I feel fine." She replied. She didn't bother mentioning the various aches from hitting the ground.

"Well the good news is the results of your CT shows you have no bleeding or a skull fracture, so we are going to keep you a few days for observation and then if you're still doing okay then you should be home by Christmas." Sebastian told her.

"Why are you caring for me, I thought you were a trauma doctor?" she inquired at Sebastian's presence.

"Oh, I am just here to keep this beast," he jerked his thumb in Jericho's direction as Jericho tried to look innocent, "from growling at the staff. He's already had one nurse sent for cultural sensitivity training and the rest of the staff is afraid to come near you."

"Jericho!" Kellista looked at him in shock only to see him shrug as if it was not important.

"Any way," Sebastian continued. "this is Doctor Klein, he is your OB/Gyn."

"OB/Gyn? Why do I need an OB/Gyn? Was I raped?" Kellista's eyes filled with tears at the thought of having been violated in such away when she was unaware.

"Sebastian!" Jericho shouted at him as he gathered Kellista up in his arms.

"No, no, no!" both of the doctors tripped over themselves trying to explain.

"You weren't raped." Jericho said to her as he rocked her in his arms. He leaned back so he could look into her tear-filled eyes and grinned. "Your pregnant."

"WHAT?!" Kellista forgot she was in a hospital as the shock of the statement hit her. She looked at Sebastian and Doctor Klein to see both of them nodding in agreement.

"Pregnant." She whispered softly. She was so wrapped up in the news the she didn't notice Sebastian and Doctor Klein stepping out of the room to give them some privacy.

Her eyes filled with happy tears this time when she looked at Jericho to see the huge smile on his face, "We are going to have a baby?" She threw her arms around him hugging him tightly despite the tubes still attached.

"I am going to be a mommy again." She bounced with joy on her bed.

"Wait until I tell my sisters. Wait until I tell my sons."

"Oh shit. I have to tell my sons." She froze, "Oh this could be bad." She knew her two younger sons would be happy for them. It was Jeremy who was going to be a hot mess.

"Yeah, well speaking of sisters. Yours are going to be here on Christmas Eve."

"What?" Jericho looked at her with a sheepish grin on his face.

"It was going to be a surprise for you, for Christmas, since your sons were spending Christmas with their father. Then I was warned not to do anything to add stress to you over the next few days. They wanted to come tonight, but since it is a nightmare to change travel arrangements and Sebastian said your condition was improving I managed to convince them to stick to the original arrangement." He kissed her cheek. "Merry Christmas, early."

"Well since we are doing early Christmas presents. Here is yours." She said to him in warning, "I planned to ask you when I saw you tonight if you would go with me to my son's Parent Meet and Greet?" she knew the timing was bad with Doctor Klein and Sebastian waiting to exam her, but she wanted to get the question out. A gesture to show him she meant for their relationship to be more permanent.

"Yes, I will go." a sigh of relief escaped Jericho.

"What was that for?" she knew this was an important event for her son, but she didn't know why Jericho felt it carried such weight.

"Ever since your phone conversation with your son I was worried you were going to go along with his plans for you to attend with that Phil*prick* guy."

"Philbrick."

"What?"

"His name is Phil*brick* not Phil*prick*." She giggled. Jericho had a way of making her laugh at the small things in life.

"Tom-a-toe, tom-o-toh." he said with a shrug. "I just didn't want you to go with Phil*brick*." he put extra emphasis on the brick part of the name. "Besides it is the first time you asked me to interact with your sons. As far as I know they don't know about us."

Kellista sighed. He was right. She had been avoiding telling her sons about Jericho, though she told her sisters Cynthia and Caleigh. They were under orders not to share information with any of the other family members.

It still caught her by surprise, how her older sisters were very supportive of her relationship with Jericho.

She thought back to the conversation with them when she first met Jericho. One of them even going as far as saying, "Get 'em young and train them right." she just rolled her eyes.

They both knew how miserable she had been with Henry and any guy who made her happy they would be happy with. They would be thrilled to hear of her and Jericho's engagement, that was going to lead to marriage.

CHAPTER TWENTY-EIGHT

KELLISTA WAS CHOMPING at the bit to go home. After already wasting her weekend here, it was time. Her sisters' plane should be landing any minute now. She didn't want to see them in the hospital. She wanted to see them at home. Jericho went to pick them up and bring them back to the hospital. He was told to look for "two slightly older, more beautiful clones of his beloved" by her sister Cynthia when he asked for a description of them.

He offered to let them stay at his house with them, but they'd never seen Kellista's little house so for the night they were going to stay at her house and then go to his house for Christmas dinner.

She was beyond ready to go. If her dang doctor did not hurry up and show up soon she would be leaving without his permission.

There was a knock on the door.

"Come in!" she yelled expecting to see her doctor.

The door opened. "Oh, it's you." her hopes were dashed when Detective Miller and Officer Wilder walked into her hospital room.

"What do you want?" she was belligerent to them. To her, grudge holding was an Olympic sport and she remember the way Detective Miller spoke to her.

"We need to make inquiries about several different things." Detective Miller spoke. He looked around the room. "Your fiancé is not with you?"

"No, do I need him? Better yet, do I need to contact my lawyer?"

"I don't think you need your lawyer, but you may need your fiancé." Detective Miller continued. "Could you please verify your address for me?"

"Why?" Kellista was in no mood to play games with the police. She wanted to get out of this hospital room. She wanted to see her sisters and she wanted to make plans with Jericho for their first Christmas together.

"Please just verify your address first." She could see Detective Miller was losing patience with her quickly. She rattled off her address watching as Detective Miller looked over at Officer Wilder.

Detective Miller cleared his throat before speaking. "Ma'am I regret to inform you that there was a fire at that location last night. Nothing could be saved."

"What?" she whispered stunned. Her little house was gone? Impossible. She just bought it. It couldn't be gone. No, her family quilt was gone. Tears started to roll down her face.

Detective Miller looked hopelessly towards Officer Wilder. Officer Wilder picked up the box of tissues and handed it to Kellista.

She took a couple to wipe her face, but it didn't stop the tears. Of all times, then Jericho and her sisters tumbled into her hospital room laughing. Jericho came to a halt at the sight of Kellista sitting on the bed crying. He rushed to her side.

"What happened?" he asked her as he gathered her up into his arms. He noticed Officer Wilder and Detective Miller standing in the room. "What the fuck are you two doing here?" he demanded.

"Jericho." he turned his attention back to a sniffling Kellista, "They were telling me my house burned down last night."

"What fucking Karma god did I piss off?" She demanded. Anger overcoming the sadness at the loss of her things.

The anger rose in her "Isn't it enough I get fucking mugged and then to top that shit off somebody burned down my fucking house."

"Don't forget your tires were slashed...." Cynthia started.

"....and sugar was put in your gas tank." Calleigh finished

"And somebody let loose a bunch of snakes in your office." Jericho added.

She looked around the room at the people. Her sisters stared at her wide-eyed. The police officer was looking at her like she was a donkey on the edge and Jericho just continued to hold her rubbing her back as he murmured soothing sounds. She knew he was trying to follow the doctor's orders for no more surprises, but something or someone was determined to ruin her Christmas. She wasn't sure she could take anything else.

Detective Miller looked up from the notes he been taking. "All these incidents have taken place over the last few months?"

"Yes." She stood up starting to gather her belongings.

The only things she had left were in her hospital room and at Jericho's house.

"We apprehended the guy who attacked you. He lawyered up as soon as we got him to the station. He is still not speaking so we have not been able to get any information out of him."

"Is there anyone you owe money to?"

"Anybody you pissed off who would hold a grudge?"

"How about your ex?"

Kellista sighed as they went into their good cop bad cop routine again.

"No, I pay all my debts."

"The only person I have pissed off lately is Delicious and we go to court right after the New Years."

"Henry didn't care about me while we were married he definitely doesn't care about me now that he is married to his Kindergartener."

She could be just as deadpan as they were in answering their questions.

"Well we will continue to look into the matter." Detective Miller said as he closed his little notebook with a snap. "Hopefully the New Year's will look better for you."

"Or I could be dead." sarcasm was her only weapon left against the tide of defeat attempting to overcome her. "Get those doctors in here so I can get the hell out of here." She knew she was being rude, but couldn't stop herself. If she was going to wallow in misery she could do it just as well at Jericho's house as she could in the hospital. Hell, she could do it better there. He at least had satellite television.

CHAPTER TWENTY-NINE

KELLISTA SAT IN the courtroom with Jessica Wield, her lawyer, sitting next to her. She didn't understand how Jessica could look so cool and composed. Kellista was a nervous wreck. She guess that was the difference between someone who worked in the courtroom for a living and someone like her who was just visiting. Jericho sat behind her looking good enough for her to lick. He managed to look absolutely gorgeous in a custom-made *Johan* suit. His friend definitely could create something fantastic.

Her mind drifted back over the holidays as she waited for the judge and Delicious to arrive. Jessica insisted they be early. "This judge," she said, "has no tolerance for lateness." She sat trying to look as cool and composed as Jessica, but failing miserably. She did get points for not fiddling with the two-carat marquise cut sapphire engagement ring Jericho gave her on New Year's Eve.

She looked down at the non-traditional stone on her left hand. The blue of the stone match Jericho's eyes perfectly. She loved it. She couldn't wait to return to work and show Nancy and April. If it were not for them dragging her out to Club Envy she would never have met Jericho and she would not be the happiest she had ever been in her life.

She had eventually started dealing with the loss of her house. She contacted the insurance company and they told her they would be in touch as soon as the police were done with their investigation.

She mourned the loss of her family pictures and the mementos from her mother. The loss of the family quilt is what truly devastated her. It was one less thing she had to pass on to one of her children.

She made it through the holidays with the support of Jericho and her sisters. The food, the laughter and the love overcame the loss of her house and belongings. It only took her a short time of being in Jericho's house to realize all she lost was a building, her home was where Jericho was at.

The police still did not have a suspect for the fire. The suspect that attacked her was not talking. Her sisters returned to their homes and life finally started to get back to normal. She had been contacted just this morning before leaving for court by the vice-president of her company. They could find no evidence to substantiate the report of her making racial slurs and he requested she return to work the following day when her vacation ended. Returning to work would help normalize things. At least as normal as they could get right now.

Now all she needed to do was make it through her arraignment with Jericho's stalker and survive the dinner with her son and then hopefully she could get on with her life with Jericho.

She had been dodging phone calls from her son and ex-husband. She figured her son told his father about Jericho being her fiancé. They've been blowing up her phone leaving voice mail after voice mail ever since she had had that conversation with Jeremy. All this time she ignored the phone calls not wanting to hear his hypocritical diatribe. She didn't need their drama on top of everything else.

She was pulled out of her thoughts with the arrival of the Judge and Bailiff. She stood with everyone else in the courtroom. She saw the District Attorney looking around nervously. She guessed someone didn't get the memo not to be late.

The door at the back of the courtroom flew open and in flounced Delicious in all of her blonde glory.

Kellista barely kept herself from rolling her eyes as Delicious's slender form, was decked out as she strolled up the aisle in four-inch heels. She stopped next to the District Attorney and shrugged out of the long coat not even paying attention to see if one of her entourage caught it before it hit the ground. She was wearing a tightly fitting dress short enough she flashed people when she sat down. Something the hordes of media people following her made sure to capture and would probably be all over the evening news.

The judge banged his gavel to get everyone's attention. "Since this is only an arraignment hearing to see if there is enough evidence to proceed to trial I will allow the media to remain. But beware if there is any type of outburst or disruption I will have every single one of you charged with contempt of court and thrown in jail." He turned a stern eye on the media crowd as they shuffled around in the back of the court room settling into seats.

Kellista saw Jericho frowning at the crowd. When one of the media tried to sit in the empty seat next to Jericho he changed his mind at the hard stare Jericho leveled on him and went to stand with the crowd at the back of the court room.

The judge gestured to the District Attorney to start.

"Your honor we feel there is enough evidence to prove Mrs. Anthony attacked the plaintiff unprovoked, causing her not only physical pain, but emotional distress which continues to affect the plaintiff to this day." He continued to drone on about all of the ills that had befallen Delicious. He flashed a smug smile at Jessica who returned it with a smile of her own.

Jessica stood up, "Your honor I am sure we can clear this matter up in just a few minutes if you would turn your attention to the video." Everyone turned to one of the several televisions placed in strategic locations around the court room affording everyone a view.

Kellista watched the familiar scene as everyone else did in the audience. She watched herself bump into Delicious, turn towards her and then turn away. She watched Delicious reach out and grab her arm. The video continued on to show Delicious swinging at Kellista and Kellista defending herself and the resulting injury Delicious suffered. Murmurs broke out from the media as they also viewed the video.

Jessica turned back to the judge when the video stopped. "As it is clearly seen in this video, my client not only attempted to walk away from Ms. Caughman, but she ended up defending herself from her, which resulted in Ms. Caughman's injury."

Jessica sat down as the district attorney jumped up. "Your Honor, this outrageous. There is no way this video could be authentic."

Jessica countered with some paperwork and a photo. "Your honor these are copies from the El Paso County

Sheriff's office showing deputies logging the security footage in as evidence. What is outrageous is that the evidence was never forwarded to my office when I requested it from the district attorney. This video is from the offsite back-up kept by Club Envy."

"In light of the evidence shown by the defense I have no choice but to rule this as a case of self-defense." The judge turned to Kellista, "Mrs. Anthony you are free to go with the courts apology." The judge ignored the stuttering of the District Attorney and the outraged yell Delicious gave at this statement.

"Court is adjourned." He announced with a bang of his gavel before exiting the court room.

At his exit, a media frenzy broke out. Question were being shouted at Delicious, Jericho, and Kellista. Jericho moved to stand next to Kellista to shield her from the enthusiastic journalists. Nobody paid attention to the nondescript guy who pushed his way to Delicious's side. Soon the crowd moved out of the court room and into the lobby.

A loud shriek echoed around the lobby of the court room. People looked around for a possible gunman until it became obvious the sound had been emitted by Delicious. Not one of dulcet tone that helped to propel her to fame no this was a sound of pure unadulterated rage. She stood next to the district attorney staring at the paper shoved into her hand with the words, "You have been served." spoken by a man who managed to blend into the crowd as if he never been there.

"You dare!" She shouted to where Jericho, Kellista, and Jessica stood surrounded by media trying to get a statement from any of them.

Everyone turned to stare to Delicious.

"You dare to threaten me with legal actions?" She shouted at Jericho, "I am Delicious. Nobody turns me down!"

"Uh oh." Kellista murmured, "Barbie doll meltdown in progress."

"You fucking bitch!" Delicious turned on Kellista, "I warned you to stay away from Jericho. HE. IS. MINE!" She shouted at Kellista.

"Actually, he is mine." Kellista calmly stated as she flashed the two-caret sapphire ring at Delicious. "He did what Beyoncé said and he put a ring on it." She knew she was pushing it with the last statement, but the devil in her couldn't resist.

Another loud shriek ranged through the lobby before Delicious launched herself at Kellista.

People backed away from the two women. Camera phones, tv cameras and other recording devices out catching the altercation on film to be played over and over again.

"Social media is going to blow up tonight." Kellista thought as she backed away from Delicious.

Jericho pushed past Kellista to stand in front of her to block the swinging Delicious. He grabbed hold of her pulling her away from Kellista, looking around for the bailiffs or police that frequent the building.

"I thought slashing your tires would be enough of a warning or even the sugar in your gas tank!" Delicious shouted as she attempted to get away from Jericho to get at Kellista. "You should be in a hole somewhere crying your fucking eyes out at the loss of your job!" The bailiff pushed through the crowd to relieve Jericho of his burden. "You should be miserable with no car or no job, not wearing my engagement ring." Delicious continued to shout as the bailiffs handcuffed her. "I am going to be Mrs. Jericho

Ryder. Not some old bitch. I got her out of the way." She continued as the bailiffs escorted her out of the area.

Jericho ushered Kellista and Jessica out of the court house. The media reporters were going crazy behind them as some rushed to follow the bailiffs taking Delicious away while others tried to get a statement from their group.

Kellista breathed a sigh of relief when they all were safely in the car speeding off from the court house. "Well, that was enough drama for me for the day." She looked around at her fellow occupants.

Jessica was just as composed now as she been in the court room, Jericho looked deep thought. "What?" She knew the look on his face. He was thinking about something hard.

"Just thinking about the things Delicious was screaming." he answered her grabbing ahold of her hand and bringing it up to his mouth.

"It is official her train has derailed especially when it comes to you. I wonder what set her off?" Kellista snuggled against Jericho.

"Probably the process server giving her a cease and desist order for her supposed engagement to Mr. Ryder?" Jessica answered, "I made sure she was served when she showed up for court today to avoid her dodging the process server."

"Wow, Jessica," Kellista looked amazed, "you are hardcore." She was full of admiration for the sleek lawyer.

"Now, if only the dinner with my son would go so smoothly." She looked up at Jericho with a faint smile.

"We have a week to prepare for that lovely event." Jericho reminded her.

"Yeah, go team." Enthusiasm thy name was not Kellista.

Chapter Thirty

KELLISTA MANAGED TO survive the week prior to her son's Parents dinner. She returned to work and got caught up on the stuff that piled up while she was on vacation. Nobody made so much as a mention of the investigation that took place while she was out. Everyone was talking about the scene occurring at the court house and the fact that none of them had been aware of Kellista's involvement in it until it started showing up on social media and airing on the news.

She was the talk of the office building. It wasn't often people got to brag they worked with the person who was responsible for the meltdown of a famous singer. Though Kellista wouldn't take credit for Delicious going over the edge it didn't stop people from pointing out her engagement was probably the last string enabling her to hang onto her sanity.

She spent the week dodging phone calls from her son Jeremy and her ex-husband Henry. It was the threat of Jericho buying her a newer more expensive phone that was keeping her from throwing her current phone when she heard the condescending and accusatory messages left by both her son and her ex. They both thought she deliberately set out to embarrass them which she found amazing. They were like two self-centered assholes in a pod. She has a few words to say to them the next time she saw them in person.

Jericho was schedule to attend a business conference in Chicago a couple of days prior to the dinner. He offered to cancel it, but Kellista vetoed the idea. He was the keynote speaker and it would be in poor form for him to cancel on such short notice. She spent the time all the way up to him going through security convincing him that she and the baby would be alright while he was gone. After all it wasn't her first pregnancy no matter her age. It wasn't the first time she would be left alone during a pregnancy. And as she like to point out to Jericho she was a grown ass woman.

Really, she did fine until the day of the Parents' dinner arrived with a huge snowstorm on the way. The day Jericho was supposed to fly home from his conference. She spoken to him the night before after the dinner learning his speech was well received. He tried to get his flight changed to return home, but there was no late-night flight. In fact, the flight he was schedule on was the earliest flight. By the time she had spoken to Jericho in the morning in Chicago, they already received two inches of snow with no end in sight. Kellista knew this was the start of a bad day.

Jericho's luck ran out at the airport. Chicago was being hit by a major snowstorm which was mucking up his plans. Flights out of O'Hare were being delayed left and right. There was no way he was going to miss getting back to the Springs. That would force Kellista to face her son and ex-husband alone. He picked up his phone to update Kellista.

There were still several hours before the dinner.

"Hey, baby. Has your flight boarded?" he heard the hope in her voice.

"Hey, darling." he couldn't stop himself from smiling at the sound of her voice. "Unfortunately, not yet. The weather is getting worse and they are talking about delaying flights."

"Oh," he heard the disappointment in her voice, "Well I would rather you be safe than attempt to get home and something happens to you. The baby and I need you."

"Don't worry. I promised I will be there and I will be there. I will see you in a few hours. I love you."

"I love you too." she said adding in kissing noises making Jericho smile, but he knew she was trying to hide the disappointment she was feeling.

This was one of the times Jericho was thankful for all of the money he made. It was time to take action.

CHAPTER THIRTY-ONE

KELLISTA SAT NERVOUSLY in the restaurant. She wasn't expecting to be the first to arrive, but she'd been ready early and the car arrived early.

She watched the news report about the storm hitting the East Coast including Chicago. She knew there would be no way for Jericho to make it back to Colorado Springs in time for the dinner especially since it started to snow in the Springs also.

Jericho had made arrangements for the car to pick her up before he left. She looked at her phone again. Nothing new came across it since she had spoken to Jericho a few hours ago. He said he would be here in time for the dinner and she truly knew he would try everything in his power, but he couldn't battle the weather.

She nervously rubbed her stomach. She was starting to show. It was earlier than she did with any of her sons. Doctor Klein wanted her to have an ultrasound. Kellista smiled at what he told her and couldn't wait to share the news with Jericho when she saw him again. She was in her own world thinking of baby clothes, the nursery and names, so she didn't hear her son arrive at the table.

"Mother." Kellista started at the sound of Jeremy's voice.

"Son." she looked up at him. She could see by the closed off expression on his face and the poorly hidden anger that it was going to be a long dinner. She wished Jericho was here with her for moral support, but she had been dealing with her son for twenty-seven years and she could handle him solo for one more night.

"You assured me you would have a dinner companion so as not to upset the number." how the hell she raised such a cold fish.

"Well I am sorry son, I have no control over the weather in Chicago."

"If you were unable to get a date I told you I arranged for Deacon Philbrick to attend." Jeremy spoke over her. She was tempted to smack the piss out of him, but since they were in an upscale restaurant and not the local bar she refrained. "Oh wait," the sarcasm was thick in his voice, "you have a fiancé, now don't you?" Jeremy made a big production of looking around, "Where is this mysterious fiancé you get into brawls over?"

She noticed his fiancé Janet was frowning at him as he spoke to her.

"Jeremy, she said he was stuck in Chicago. You saw the news before we left. You know they are getting a large winter storm on the east coast and flights were being delayed." She quietly admonished him.

Kellista saw Jeremy face soften as she spoke. At least he showed real emotion towards Janet. She would have been truly concerned if he treated her as coldly as he treated Kellista, but he seemed to genuinely care for her and she was happy for them.

She was saved from being berated further by the arrival of Janet's parents. She met them prior, but this would be the first time since her divorce from Henry they would be together.

Before she could enjoy their presence Henry and his new wife arrived.

"Kellista." Now she remembers where Jeremy got his coldness as Henry greeted her.

"Henry."

"You remember my wife, Randi?" he introduced her as he helped her into a seat between Jeremy and him.

"Yes, I do. Hello, dear." she greeted her with her sweetest smile, "How is Kindergarten?" she mumbled softly to herself.

Jeremy gave her a sharp look and she looked back at him in total innocence. Janet smothered a laugh under her breath.

The waiter came to take the drink orders. She bristled as Henry order a glass of wine for her without even consulting her.

She stopped the waiter.

"I will have a glass of sparkling water with a slice of lemon." she ordered in place of the wine.

Henry and Jeremy both gave her a strange look. While Janet's mother looked at her with a questioning look on her face. Kellista gave her a sly wink and received a wide grin in return.

Janet's mother mouthed "Congratulations!" to Kellista and continued on with the conversation without giving anyone else a hint of their unspoken words.

The small talk continued as everyone looked over the menus. Once their orders for food were placed, Jeremy started speaking.

"As you are aware Janet has agreed to marry me?" he started. "We have decided to hold the wedding down here in the Springs instead up in Denver because this is where Janet grew up and both her parents and Mother resides here."

Kellista could see the happy smile on Janet's face as Jeremy spoke. "We decide to have the wedding in mid-June and Janet was hoping you would help her and her mother plan it, Mother." Jeremy looked at her as he spoke. From his tone of voice, she knew it was not his idea.

She bit her lip at this information. She wanted to help in the planning of her oldest son's wedding, but she had no idea how to tell him she might not be able to tend the event do to the birth of his new sibling. She was saved from any comment due to a commotion at the front of the restaurant. Kellista looked up to see Jericho rushing towards the table ignoring the maître de who was trying to fawn over his arrival.

She stood up in surprise, not containing the huge smile of joy from crossing her face at his arrival. She didn't think anything about their audience when he swept her up into his arms kissing her.

Chapter Thirty-Two

Jericho couldn't contain his happiness at seeing Kellista sitting at the table surrounded by three other couples. His heart managed to beat faster at the sight of the huge smile crossing her face.

He couldn't stop himself from sweeping her up into his arms and kissing her. His pent-up desire and love for her transmitted to her in that one kiss. His cock grew stiff as he felt her soft body against his as she sunk into the kiss. It was only the repeated sounds of the word "Mother!"

bringing them back to reality.

Jericho lifted his mouth from Kellista. The look of her swollen lips was almost too much to resist.

"Hello, darling." he spoke to her softly ignoring everyone else. The intimate greeting become second nature by this time.

"Hi, Jericho," she smiled at him, "I missed you and so did the baby." She whispered as she took his hand and placed it on the bulge that was their child.

"Mother, who is this guy?" A man's voice demanded from behind Kellista as he reached out and tried to pull her away from Jericho.

Son or no son, no one put their hands on Kellista.

"I am the guy who is going to break your arm if you don't get your damn hands off of her." Jericho didn't try to keep the menace out of his voice. The look of anger in his eyes spoke of the bodily harm he was going to commit in the next few seconds if this guy didn't remove his hand fast.

Jeremy must have seen something on Jericho's face told him he meant business because his hand dropped from Kellista's arm quicker than lightening.

Jericho couldn't stop his eyes from roaming over Kellista as she spoke to her son. She changed a little in the few days since he seen her, but the glow of impending motherhood covered her like a warm coat. She glowed with an inner beauty.

He tuned back into the argument taking place while he been doing a visual examination of Kellista. He wrapped his arms around her, unable to stop from cuddling her as she spoke to the male members of her family. He didn't interfere, but his touch let her know that he was there for support.

"This is Jericho. My fiancé." She informed them. He smiled as she introduces her to the male member of her family. "I told you before I was engaged." She showed them the two-carat sapphire on her left hand.

"Oh my god congratulations!" Janet squealed as she pulled Kellista out of Jericho's arms for a big hug. Jericho could see the surprise on her face as both Janet and the lady he assumed was her mother hugged her and babbled their congratulations.

All hell broke loose from her son and the older man who resembled him who he assumed was her ex-husband, Henry.

"Fiancé?!" her son exclaimed, "I thought you were joking."

"And? How is it my fault you didn't believe me?" Kellista responded.

"Well that's disgusting." Jeremy stuttered.

"Disgusting. Disgusting?" Kellista yelled at her son.

"Yes, disgusting." Her ex-husband echoed her son. "He has got to be half your age."

"You stand there with that pre-school drop out and dare to tell me my marrying Jericho is disgusting?" She turned on Henry her face covered with outrage at their double standard. Then she turned to her son Jeremy.

"Jericho is five years older than you are Jeremy where as your father's wife Randi is two years younger than you are. You explain to me why it is okay for your father, but disgusting when it comes to me?"

Jericho rubbed Kellista's back, as she ripped her son a new one, in hopes of getting her to calm down. He knew her getting this angry wasn't good for her or the baby.

"Well it is obvious he is only with you for your money." Jeremy stated.

"What money?" Kellista demanded. "I have a burnt down house that I am still paying the mortgage on and a ten-year-old car. What fucking money do I have?"

"Well the money you get from dad for the divorce. Your alimony."

"For your information Jeremy. The only money I got from divorcing your father is my half of the house. And as for alimony I don't get any alimony."

"Yes, you do. Father has been telling me your demands for alimony is causing his business to lose money and is why he is unable to help me and Janet pay for our wedding." Jeremy stated. "As a matter of fact, he is thinking about selling it since you are draining so much money out of it."

"I don't know why your father's business is losing money, but it is not because of me. Have you ever thought that your father is just a cheap ass and not willing to help you pay for your wedding?"

"Besides there is no way he is after her for her money." the statement came from an unexpected source. Henry's new wife, Randi, was supporting Kellista. Everyone's mouth dropped open in shock at the statement from her. She continued on not even aware of the shock she caused, "He is Jericho Ryder. He is like a Kajillionaire." She stated as she took a bite of her dinner salad calmly continuing her dinner as the drama unfolded around her.

Kellista didn't know if she was that cool of a customer or just oblivious of what was going on around her or just didn't give a fuck?

All eyes turned towards Jericho. He gave a slight smile, "B. not K" he said.

"What?" Henry and Jeremy demanded.

"I am a Billionaire, not a Kajillionaire." He stated. The

stunned expressions on their faces was worth the bomb he just dropped on them.

Kellista turned towards an older couple and spoke, "I am sorry to have to cut our dinner short. I hope we can get together at a future date." She then turned to a young woman who hugged and congratulated her. "Janet good luck in your marriage to my son. In light of the fact that I shall be due to have my babies around the time of your wedding I am going to have to decline your invitation to help plan your wedding."

She inclined her head towards Jeremy, Henry and Randi. Grabbing ahold of Jericho's hand she started towards the door to front of the restaurant.

"You are not going to ruin my plans!" Jericho heard the shout come from behind them. What the fuck now, he thought turning to look behind him.

Chapter Thirty-Three

KELLISTA AND JERICHO both turned in surprise in time to see her ex-husband, Henry, picked up a steak knife and was preparing to stab someone. No. Not someone he was preparing to stab Kellista.

"For years I put up with your disdain and your trying to turn my sons against me. I finally found someone to love me and I couldn't support her because of you!" A crazed look entered his eyes as he swung the knife in Kellista's direction.

Jericho pushed Kellista behind him whispering, "You never mentioned your ex-husband was crazy."

"I didn't know!" she answered back. Slowly she moved behind his body, protecting her stomach from her crazy knife-swinging ex-husband. She barely acknowledged the fact that she bumped into his current wife who managed to slip past the knife to safety.

"If you would just die then I could sell the business for millions and I would be able to support Randi in the style she needs." Jericho grabbed the arm swinging the knife in their direction as Henry kept ranting.

"I tried to make it look like an accident with those snakes, but no that didn't work!" He swung wildly at Jericho, his eyes contained a wild look, spittle flew out of his mouth as he confessed his sins.

He lunged. Jericho kept moving back waiting for an opening to try to disarm him. Everyone else stood back out of the way of the madman.

"Even that fucking guy I hired to mug you didn't kill you like I paid him to." Jericho snatched a metal tray out of the hand of a waiter who was hiding behind a table as the rest of the staff cleared the restaurant. "He took my money and didn't complete the job. What kind of customer service is that?" Henry demanded of the people who were trapped by his swinging knife as if he expected an answer.

"If you just fucking died I could have sold my business for millions and not have to split the money with you. Randi and I could be living on the beach in Jamaica or somewhere where it didn't fucking snow."

"Why don't you just die you fucking bitch?" Henry screamed at Kellista as Jericho swung the tray hitting Henry's hand that was holding the knife. Jericho kicked out with his leg connecting with the paunch that was Henry's stomach doubling him over. A powerful upper cut connected Jericho's fist with Henry's jaw knocking Henry back, spinning him around to collapse on their table amongst the dishes of food.

"Henry was the one responsible for burning down my house," Kellista stated watching Henry slumped to the ground.

She let out a gasp as she was unexpectedly grabbed from behind. "No, I was the one to set your house on fire." Randi said as she held a knife to Kellista's throat.

"You? But why?" Kellista gasped out. Jericho was too far away from her to stop Randi.

A voice colder and harder than the soft-spoken voice she used in the past emerged from Randi, "It's like Henry said. He could have sold the business for millions, but your divorce decree stated he had to give you half of the proceeds. Well I am too greedy to share so we decided to get rid of you." She told Kellista as she pressed the point of the sharp dinner knife into Kellista's throat drawing blood.

"Randi, did Henry every tell you about my singing career?" Kellista gasped out as she reached up to grab ahold of the hand choking her.

"Singing?" the question momentarily distracted Randi enough that Kellista she was able to bring her elbow back to solidly strike Randi in the solar plexus following with slamming her heel into her in-step.

The pain caused Randi to loosen her grip on the knife and Kellista was able to slam her knee into her groin knowing the movement caused just as much pain in a female as it did in a male. Evidence by Randi bending in half as she clutched her wounded vagina. With her head, down and in striking distance Kellista slammed her knee into Randi's nose, breaking the other female nose just as the police rushed into the restaurant, having been called by the maître de.

A pair of police officers cuffed an unconscious Henry as another set of officers started gathering a crying Randi from the floor. "I guess I spelled Sign instead of Sing." Kellista stated as they took Randi away to seek medical care and arrest her.

"Are you alright?" Jericho demanded as he pressed a napkin to the small bleeding cut in her throat as Detective Miller and Officer Wilder approached them. Other officers were collecting statements from those people who were unable to escape the restaurant when Henry started swinging with the knife.

"Well, better late than never." Jericho put into words everyone thoughts as the police arrived after the threat was over.

"We were actually on our way to see you at your home to report we finally gotten the mugging suspect to talk and that he named Henry Anthony, Mrs. Anthony's ex-husband, as the person who hired him." Detective Miller informed Jericho. "With his statement and the statement of all of the people in the restaurant tonight we will have enough evidence to convict him and the new Mrs. Anthony of arson and the attempted murder of Mrs. Anthony."

"Don't forget to charge them both with assault on a pregnant woman under the fetal homicide laws of Colorado." Jeremy uttered this statement. Now that was a surprise, full of unexpected support. "Mom, just informed us she was pregnant with a baby."

"Babies." Kellista mumbled lifting her face from Jericho's shoulder.

"Babies?" everyone exclaimed.

She looked up into Jericho's blue eyes. "Yes babies, we are having twin boys." She told Jericho. A wide delighted grin spread across his face. He scooped Kellista up into his arms. "We are getting married and I am never letting you out of my sight again." He declared as his mouth closed over hers.

"I am going to be the best daddy ever!" he told her when he lifted his mouth from hers.

"I know you will. That is why I love you." Kellista told him as she stared into his eyes, seeing the love shining in them.

"I love you for now and always." Jericho whispered to her.

A clearing throat sounded behind them. Jericho turned with Kellista still in his arms to see her son standing behind her holding his fiancé hand. "Mom." he started off sheepishly. He looked down at his shoes like he did when he was a little boy before squaring his shoulders and looking Kellista in the face. "Mom, I am sorry. Sorry for believing the shit dad told me about you and for the way I have been treating you since the divorce."

A smile cracked Kellista's face as she caught a glimpse of the loving boy she raised and not the asshole that taken over his body lately. "I forgive you, Jeremy." She raised her arms to hug him from the comfort of Jericho's arms.

"I would love to be a part of my new brothers' lives, please." He whispered into her hair.

"Always." she sniffled. Overcome with emotions. She was getting her son back and she was having more sons. Jericho was in her life and she could never be happier.

EPILOGUE

IT WAS FINALLY OVER.

The yelling.

The screaming.

The cries for drugs.

In the aftermath, the cooing of the new babies could be heard.

It's been touch and go for a few minutes there. He was positive Sebastian almost gave into his demands for drugs and was sure he was going to sedate him instead of Kellista, but Kellista's OB/Gyn overruled him.

Kellista came through the birth of their twins like a champ, it was Jericho who fell apart. The constant pain of labor was hard for him to watch. Not even the squeezing that Kellista did to his hand made up for her suffering. A suffering no longer obvious as she sat in the Birthing Center bed staring with the same fascination on her face Jericho had on his at their new daughters.

All of a sudden it hit him and Jericho sat down abruptly. He was now a father.

He was now a father to twin girls.

Girls.

What did he know about raising girls. He been expecting boys. He looked up to see Kellista smiling at him over the top of his daughter's head.

"It's going to be all right. You will get the hang of it."

Jericho stood up and pressed a kiss to the top of the daughter's head he was holding "Hello little darling." He repeated the greeting to the daughter that Kellista was holding and finally pressing one to Kellista's lips this one was a long, deep loving kiss.

"With you by my side, I can do anything. Including being the best husband and father ever."

"I love you." Kellista whispered to him.

"I will love you for always and beyond." He whispered back before capturing her mouth with his.

JERICHO

ABOUT THE AUTHOR

I LIVE IN FOUNTAIN, Colorado with my husband and two kids. I have been writing all of my life. I became addicted to romance novels when I was teenager thanks to my mother's love of reading. I wrote my first romance novel when I was in junior high school. I decided to stop hiding my desire to write and to just go for it.

Thank you for reading my book. I hope you enjoyed reading it as much as I did writing it. Stay tune there is more to come. Sign up for my Newsletter and follow me on Facebook and Twitter. Please consider leaving a review.

Twitter: @MissSassy714
Facebook: Author Donna R. Mercer
Amazon: Donna Mercer
www.DonnaRMercer.com

JETICHO

175

JERICHO

Made in the USA
Columbia, SC
02 February 2023